The End of the World Might
Not Have Taken Place

Patrik Ouředník

THE END OF THE WORLD MIGHT NOT HAVE TAKEN PLACE

Translated from the French by Alexander Hertich

DALKEY ARCHIVE PRESS

McLean, IL / Dublin

Originally published by Éditions Allia as *La fin du monde n'aurait pas eu lieu* in 2017.

Copyright © by Patrik Ouředník in 2019.

Translation copyright © by Alexander Hertich, 2019.

First Dalkey Archive edition, 2019.

Library of Congress Control Number: 2019955148

www.dalkeyarchive.com
McLean, IL / Dublin

Printed on permanent/durable acid-free paper.

Contents

Translator's Note

"It is to be hoped the time will come, thank God, in some circles it already has, when language is best used where it is most efficiently abused."
— Samuel Beckett,
Letter to Axel Kaun, 9 July 1937

LIKE THE NOVEL'S narrator, Patrik Ouředník is both a writer and translator in real life. *The End of the World Might Not Have Taken Place* is his second work originally written in French. His other books, including his most well-known novel, *Europeana* (published by Dalkey Archive Press in 2005), first appeared in Czech. Over the past thirty-five years he has also translated a number of infamously thorny texts from authors such as Samuel Beckett, Raymond Queneau, and François Rabelais from French into Czech, and Vladimír Holub and Ivan Wernisch from Czech into French.

This short literary biography is important, for it helps provide some context to Ouředník's relationship with language. As a non-native speaker of French (while his mother did speak to him in French during his childhood, he didn't really learn the language until moving to France in 1984), his writing exhibits a fascination with the peculiarities of words and their shifting meanings and obscure subtleties that most native speakers take for granted. He has a translator's ear with a keen interest in how words and sentences can follow each other smoothly, or not. This is amplified by the ludic quality of his novel, which is filled with double entendres, portmanteau words, puns, and intentional malapropisms.

One of the novel's most striking linguistic characteristics is the use of differing registers. Like Queneau, who frequently juxtaposed philosophical or mock-epic styles with everyday language and pronunciation, among many other linguistic feats (for example his work *Exercises in Style*, which tells the same uneventful story in 99 different ways—including "Alexandrines," "Cross-Examination," "Parechesis," "Olfactory," and "Rhyming Slang"—and which Ouředník translated into Czech in 1985), in *The End of the World Might Not Have Taken Place* Ouředník mixes intentionally neutral, journalistic prose, slang, abstruse sesquipedalianism, and vulgarity with technical vocabulary (which may not always be precisely correct, scientifically) and archaic expressions to great comic effect. A prime example of this is found in the explanation of the expression "gee, ain't that swell" from the chapter "Phrases to Remember in this Book." The narrator discusses his fondness for out-of-date expressions: "Their desuetude touches me. They no longer have a place among us, they're as dead as the people we loved." In French the paragraph ends, "*D'aucuns comprendront,*" which, in its most straightforward, literal sense, means "some will understand." However, in modern French "*aucun*" is a negation meaning "no" when used with a noun, "*je n'ai aucune idée*" (I have no idea). According to the *Dictionnaire historique de la langue française*, the use of "*aucun*" initially had a positive sense when it was introduced into French around 950. It then took on a negative meaning in the following century, which it continues to have today. However, it was also rarely used in a positive sense with the plural "*aucuns*," perhaps most notably by Rabelais in the 16th century; by the time Victor Hugo used the word in *Les Misérables* it was already considered archaic.

Most contemporary readers would not know this and would have difficulty understanding the sentence. Therefore, translating the phrase simply as "some will understand" misses the texture, anachronism, and ludic quality of the original, which is the point of the tag line. After much consternation I translated the sentence as "Some will understumble, others wonnot," adapting the sentence's original wording while conserving its intent. "Understumble" is originally from Jonathan Swift. I felt this word for "understand" worked well. It is out of date, as is "wonnot," an obsolete form of won't. More interestingly, we find here a playful combination of understanding and stumbling (not understanding)—just like original readers may stumble over the archaic word in a paragraph discussing outdated expressions.

Because of this frequent word play, some of the solutions to the linguistic hurdles encountered during the translation of the novel come directly from or were inspired by the authorized Czech translation of the book, which Ouředník reviewed and approved. While liquor brands such as Pernod and Ricard do exist, Scrue does not, for example. A real brand, Suze, used in the original fictive French advertising slogan, "Suze-moi," didn't work directly for the lewd pun in English.

When translating, my objective, to borrow from Mark Polizzotti's *Sympathy for the Traitor: A Translation Manifesto*, "is to offer readers the best likeness of the work that I can, retaining the quirks and personality of the original, but also making sure my version affords literary enjoyment *in English*—even if that involves a certain creative license." Ultimately, a translation should sound good. To use a hackneyed expression, it should flow. However, as Ouředník explained during an exchange we had about the linguistic pitfalls in this novel, he does not want the text to flow *too* well. It should, at times, grate and squeak. There needs to be some sand in the Vaseline. Just like the novel's content, with its biting social criticism, the language should also be subversive. It should give you pause and encourage you to stop and reflect on what we say and why we say it, perhaps even with a smile on your face.

Have you had your breakfast yet?

Alexander Hertich, 2019

The End of the World Might Not Have Taken Place

Patrik Ouředník

ENCOUNTER

JEAN-PIERRE DURANCE EMERGED from the train station and was heading toward the bus stop on the other side of Boulevard Montparnasse when he saw, at a sidewalk café, a back that looked familiar. The man with the back was Gaspard, and he will be the main character of this book. Jean-Pierre Durance's part, on the other hand, will quickly fade. You don't need to remember his name.

Durance walked around the table to make sure that it really was Gaspard, Gaspard Boisvert, a little over six feet tall, broad-shouldered, salt-and-pepper hair, early sixties. He then said, "Hello, Gaspard." They knew each other only vaguely. They'd met two or three times, and there was a time, fifteen or twenty years ago, when he certainly would have said, "Hello, Mr. Boisvert." But this was an age of first names, it was more personal, friendly, direct, more international, too. The whole world had become a conglomerate of first names.

Gaspard raised his head. He seemed to recognize his interlocutor.

"Hello, what are you doing here?"

"Oh," Durance responded, "just in town on biz."

It was also an age of abbreviations.

"I'm heading back to Orléans tonight. But what about you? What are you up to? I heard you were back for good? I mean back in France? Nothing else tempting you across the pond, in the U.S. of A., as they say?"

In the United States Gaspard had served as an advisor to the

stupidest American President in history. It had been more than
ten years ago, but every time he ran into someone he knew, that
person felt entitled to ask the same questions. His American
interlude had bestowed upon him, once and for all, his social
identity.

This was, moreover, another reason for Durance to call
Gaspard "Gaspard" rather than Mr. Boisvert: advising the stupidest American President in history was nothing to sneeze at.
Maybe I could invite myself to sit down, Durance said to himself, I've got forty-five minutes.

"That's correct."

"May I sit down? I've got forty-five minutes."

With his hand Gaspard gestured toward the chair across from
him.

"What have you been up to since your return? I imagine
you've had some interesting offers. Advising the American
President is nothing to sneeze at. Especially for a Frenchman."

"That's true."

"You should write a book. A kind of behind-the-scenes
account. It would sell like hotcakes."

"Yes, it would."

Durance sensed a slight uneasiness. Gaspard's answers were
not falling within the conversational norms of good-natured
individuals.

"Do you come here often?"

"Every day."

"Do you live around here? Sorry if I'm intruding."

"In a hotel nearby, yes."

"Oh, in a hotel."

"Nearby, yes."

"My wife will be thrilled to know I ran into you. It must be
at least fifteen years, right? Even more?"

"No doubt."

In order to spare the reader from tedious dialogue, let's sum-
marize: the two men stayed on the terrace for a good half hour.
Unsettled by Gaspard's offhand attitude, Durance had become
even more insistent, as happens in such situations. Why, pardon

my curiosity, in a hotel, why not enter the diplomatic corps, such an astonishing career, by the way, he and his wife, they were immediately impressed. Did he remember their friend, what was his name again? And so on.

After his business conference, Durance returned to the train station. Passing the café again he noted that Gaspard's back was still there. This time he did not approach him.

Here Jean-Pierre Durance's role comes to an end.

THE FUTURE OF THE WORLD

THE FUTURE ISN'T what it used to be. You must have noticed this yourself: the future isn't what it used to be.

In the past, the future mainly unfolded in one of the following ways:

(1) The world would end, and everything would start again from scratch, with the creation of an identical world—the pessimistic version of most belief systems.

(2) The world would end in a horrifying and final bloodbath, from which would arise a world of bliss—the optimistic version of some religions.

(3) The world would never end, and bliss, which acted as the leavening agent, would continue to increase until the end of days, which were themselves infinitely extendable—the foolhardy version of the ends of History.

But by the beginning of the twenty-first century such theories had run their course. Forecasts had changed. All people endowed with a certain understanding of the facts on the ground agreed on one point: no matter how you imagine it, it's going to end badly. Either in a horrible bloodbath followed by nothing at all—the optimistic hypothesis. Or by bloodbaths here and there, followed by further bloodbaths here and there, without end, until the universe expands to the point that its density reaches an infinite value, which would in turn precipitate the destruction of the galaxies and the poor miserable wretches who live there. Some observers added a supplementary aspect: a concomitant and heretofore inconceivable dulling of humanity.

GASPARD, OR OPTIMISM

GASPARD WAS NO STUPIDER than anyone else. He imagined the future much as you and I would. But his education impelled him to act as if nothing were wrong. He had the gift, or the weakness, of occasionally disregarding what he knew for certain, such that for several hours, for a whole day, a cautious optimism would come over him. What if you could influence the way of the world? So that man could realize his varied abilities, engendering within him an irrevocable desire for peace, making him love his brother, making love triumph over his greediness, his egotism, his natural meanness? Inaugurating a peaceful coexistence, with people living in harmony, but which, at the same time, would not prevent creativity or imagination from blossoming? Protecting mankind from pure necessity, making work pleasant, granting a peaceful death to all, preventing the universe from expanding?

GASPARD AND THE BOMBING

GASPARD WAS BORN on 13 February 1955, on the tenth anniversary of the bombing of the German city of Dresden by Allied forces. The Germans and the Allies were at war back then. Later, by the time Gaspard was born, the Allies and most Germans had also become allies. He was born in a small village in the flat, gloomy countryside of northern France. I don't recall the village's name. His older sister died in an accident at the age of five, when he was three. Now the only child in a relatively well-to-do family, he felt the vague desire to please, as best he could, his parents, who were traumatized by what the neighbors called their family tragedy. Up to the age of fourteen or fifteen he would speak to his dead sister and ask her advice. Then he stopped speaking to her. High school in Lille, then university studies in Anglo-American Literature and Culture at the Sorbonne in Paris. His thesis, which he never completed, examined three of four novels by an American writer from the 1930s, Nathanael West: *Miss Lonelyhearts, A Cool Million*, and *The Day of the Locust*. The thesis shows an evolution in West's writing: in the first novel America is heading steadily toward ruin, in the second it's plunging into a nightmare, the third ends on the brink of the Apocalypse. The end of the world already. After quitting school he spent nearly three years in the United States, where he met up with some people from the underground—what else. It was during this time that he also met the niece of the future President of the United States, an encounter that would later change his life for several months. They met at a rock concert.

Where else.

In those amiable days, America fought against communism and Soviet imperialism in the name of democracy and the free market, and communism fought against American imperialism and capitalism in the name of the proletariat and the end of History. The rest of the world had but limited importance.

Back in France, Gaspard began working as a translator. Besides the immeasurable amount of dross that his editors had him translate, he had been successful in imposing on them several authors who were dear to his heart: Donald Barthelme, Joan Didion, Richard Brautigan, and Kurt Vonnegut. Vonnegut was the author of a book on the bombing of Dresden, *Slaughterhouse-Five*. The bombing of Dresden had killed more people than the atomic bomb dropped six months later on the Japanese city of Hiroshima, but it was lesser-known. Those deaths were the result of an ordinary weapon. The atomic bomb on the other hand was sublimely spectacular, and it's in the nature of spectacular things to be more enthralling than a simple death toll. For every death during the twentieth century, on average 2.55 human lives appeared on Earth, whereas the spectacles that left a lasting impression on the imagination were, when all was said and done, few and far between.

That night approximately 100,000 people were killed in the Dresden bombings.

For the first time 255,000 newborns cried out in fear.

But Gaspard had not yet been born.

BIG BERTHA AND ME

Now AS FOR ME, I was born on the twelfth day of August on the forty-fifth anniversary of the day that Big Bertha, a cannon with a range of 12.5-kilometers, was put into service. This happened in 1914. At the time the Germans and the Allies were at war. An eminently modern war—people had noticed that the more the cannons, the fewer the casualties. Over the course of several months the number of cannons increased while the casualties decreased. This perturbed several conservative generals but pleased the troops. Except the equipment that brought about the reduction in losses contributed, by its very essence, to prolonging war and therefore to increasing losses. All things considered, a good old brawl with sabers or machetes is definitely much more charitable.

I was born in Prague, a city dear to those whose souls, in order to flourish, require decadence. It was the capital of a country whose name is impossible to remember: Czechoslovakia. Too long—once it has more than three syllables, unless you've won or lost an important war, a country doesn't exist.

THE BOMBING OF DRESDEN

PERHAPS THE BOMBING of Dresden didn't result in 100,000 dead. Other sources indicate different numbers. Accordingly, if we trust the Red Cross humanitarian organization, there were 305,000. If we believe the German officer in charge of the cleanup, 221,500. If we take the conclusions of the German newspaper *Die Welt* into account, between 60 and 65,000. If we prefer another German daily, *Süddeutsche Zeitung,* around 300,000. If we consult the Dresden police report compiled after the bombings, 135,000. If we refer to the one written by the government of the German Democratic Republic, 35,000. If we turn to the work of a commission of experts from the Soviet army, 250,000. If we give credit to the German Minister of Public Enlightenment and Propaganda, 200,000. If we place confidence in a commission of German historians, between 18 and 25,000, but another German historian puts the number at 40,000.

In short, between 18,000 and 305,000. Thus, the possibility that there were 100,000, plus or minus a few, is in accordance with all known data points.

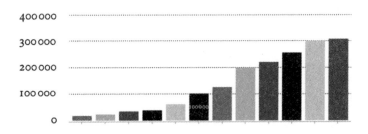

WHAT I KNOW ABOUT GASPARD

NOTWITHSTANDING THE WARM REGARD we felt for one another, we had spent rather little time together. Say somewhere around thirty meetings, which would make for somewhere between 150 and 200 hours of conversation—more friendly than intimate, tending toward general more than private matters. Most of what I know about Gaspard I gleaned from what one might call his diary if it weren't for the fact that these were just loose leaves, some dated, others not, randomly collected in two plywood suitcases, the kind of suitcase that, long ago, you'd see young people carrying when they left the countryside to move to Paris, or when they were drafted and went to join their regiments. All kinds of papers in all kinds of shapes and sizes covered with memories, reflections, aphorisms, minor observations—"*Today, Monday March 2, I noticed that my ophthalmologist has the head of a toad*"—now obsolete notes—"*Euro / Franc: divide by 3 + multiply by 20*"—newspaper clippings, excerpts from books, or short poems:

> *Splitting its shell hole a crack*
> *the dream pierces the black.*
> *The pale mien*
> *of being boiled in a blood-filled tureen.*

There were also some report cards, old photos, postcards, and even several of his parents' love letters from before they were married. In short, something like *disjecta membra,* but which nonetheless allowed me to piece together several scenes of the Gaspardian life.

MY PROJECTS

WRITING A BOOK about the end of the world was a longstanding project. I'd already written a play on the same subject. It was called *Yesterday and the Day After Tomorrow*. But you're obsessed, my wife said when I mentioned the idea of taking another crack at it.

I don't think so. But I might be wrong. According to psychologists, the idea of the end of the world allows people to accept their own mortality. What's more, the world doesn't even have to end. They say the death of others in and of itself is soothing. To be on your deathbed and to be able to say, *In any case, this is going to happen to all those stupid bastards*, would bring peace to the soul.

Just as long as you don't believe in the afterlife. Imagine! Just imagine! To run into all of them again!

MY EDITOR

As for my editor, he sniggered. The end of the world? His tone betrayed his thoughts: a rather hackneyed subject. Ever since the last end of the world, no one has believed in it anymore.

"But this time it's for real."

"Ah, you've got some inside information?"

Increasingly ironic.

"You might say that. I've read some reports about it. Everything dependable."

"It doesn't sell anymore. You're going to need to spice it up with something less mundane."

"The end of the world is never mundane."

"More appealing, then. I don't know . . . a family secret, for example."

"That's the plan."

"Something about religion."

"Also the plan."

"With one or two wars as a backdrop."

"There are tons of them."

"A dictator. People like that."

"It's human nature."

"The bloodier it is, the more they'll like it."

"Even more human."

"Take Hitler for example. An age-old subject, but it still sells."

"I'm aware of that."

"But don't forget current affairs, of course."

"Of course."

"Something along the lines of the past resurfacing under the troubling auspices of today."

"Nicely said."

"Not too much sex . . . it slows down the pace."

"Not too much."

"A few biblical references."

"That goes without saying."

My editor would have made a pitiful writer.

Just as bad as the rest of them.

THE FOLLOWING CHAPTERS

THE FOLLOWING CHAPTERS treat of family secrets, wars, divine action, and bloodthirsty dictators.

GASPARD AND THE FAMILY SECRET

GASPARD'S GRANDFATHER may have been of Austrian origin. At least that's what his father maintained. This in spite of official documents that clearly indicated a French line of descent: Boisvert, Jean-Baptiste, born 8 June 1876 in Cassel, Maritime Flanders province, brown hair and eyebrows, brown eyes, normal forehead, average nose, average mouth, round chin, oval face. But Gaspard's father had a secret.

COMPUTER PROGRAMS

IN THE OLD DAYS the French had an expression: "to be one war behind." It meant not being up to date on the latest events—the last presidential election, the evolution of sexual mores, developments in the areas of fashion and technology. During the twentieth and twenty-first centuries, however, the expression had lost its relevance: there were too many wars and they followed each another too closely. Live media coverage only added to the confusion. Except for a few military strategists, no one was up to date.

Then some computer programs were released with modules that could announce the start of a new war by emitting a specific sound. The default was BOOM! but it was possible to choose another among the following options:

CRASH!
WHACK!
WHAM!
BANG!
THUMP!
BADABOOM!
OUCH!

Or:

Some jokers had then hacked into the module to add: HA, HA, HA!

GOD AND GODLESS CITIES

THE FIRST BOMBING recorded in human history was God's airstrike against four cities in the Jordan River plain, the most famous of which was Sodom. The event is recounted in the holy book of the Jews. The inhabitants of Sodom lived in great sin. The men took pleasure in penetrating each other. God sent two angels to inspect. They confirmed the charges: after inquiring as to their genders, the inhabitants wanted to defile the angels. The Eternal consequently made fire and brimstone rain down upon Sodom. There were three survivors: the prophet Lot, known for his fondness for cheap wine, and his two daughters. His wife could have escaped the disaster as well, but, hearing cries, she turned around while fleeing. She was transformed into a pillar of salt. God wanted no witnesses.

There were no survivors in the three other cities of Gomorrah, Admah, and Zeboim.

GASPARD'S GRANDFATHER

"IT'S NOT ONE-HUNDRED PERCENT certain," said Boisvert, Pierre-Maurice, to his son Boisvert, Gaspard. "I'm not saying that. But there's a possibility."

Gaspard's father was more or less convinced that he was the fruit of a night of love between his mother and a certain German army lance corporal by the name of Adolf Hitler. His was one of the most famous names in world history: in the space of a few years Adolf had managed to kill by proxy some sixty million individuals. He was considered the greatest and most skilled murderer of all time. With an average of 22,810 dead per day, he was well ahead of his main rivals: the Soviet Stalin (10,163), the Chinese Mao Zedong (9,904), the Japanese Hirohito (5,562), the Turkish Enver (2,857), and the Cambodian Pol Pot (1,574). All by themselves, those six were casually able to wipe out 8.5% of the world population.

	RANK	PER DAY	PER HOUR	%
	I	22 810	950,5	43
	2	10 163	423,5	19
	3	9 904	412,75	19
	4	5 562	231,75	11
	5	2 857	119	5
	6	1 574	65,5	3

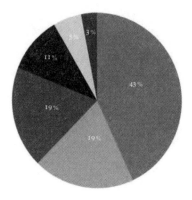

The night of love in question supposedly took place in August 1918, in what would later become the suburbs of Lille.

Pierre-Maurice obtained this information from his mother. "One day I was down at the river doing the laundry. On the other side a German soldier was drawing on a piece of thick cardstock he had on his lap. I was curious as to what he was drawing."

"I'd like to be wrong about this," said Pierre-Maurice. "If I'm talking to you about it, it's because you need to watch out if you start to get ideas. Heredity exists, whatever they may say."

PHRASES TO REMEMBER IN THIS BOOK

I HAVE DECIDED to introduce several phrases into my book that will reappear more or less regularly. They will have two functions: to confirm you're still reading the same story and to give you the opportunity to pause, to reflect on what happened previously in the book and more generally on the meaning of human destiny. I will choose among:

1. Gee, ain't that swell.
2. A dog's life.
3. So it goes.
4. Lil' Luck.
5. Do you *or* do we have a choice?
6. It seemed important at the time.
7. The choice is yours.

Gee, ain't that swell. To give the era a voice and therefore more directly to attain intemporality would have required a more modern expression. But as a matter of course I prefer old-fashioned expressions to new ones. Their desuetude touches me. They no longer have a place among us, they're as dead as the people we loved. By exhuming them, I'm not doing them any favor. They seem even stupider than they were before. But not to me. To me, they're just as stupid as they were then. Some will understumble, others wonnot.

A dog's life used to symbolize a life that was barely worth that of a dog, the life of dogs who were subject to their masters, self-important and stubborn when facing the animal world. The expression persisted, more or less, down to my own time, even if it no longer made much sense. Dogs, in the society I lived in, were treated better than most humans on Earth. But where reality fizzles out, metaphor takes over. *A dog's life* will be used here to highlight the life of those subjugated to the vagaries of fate.

So it goes will have the strong potential of bringing people together. The author refuses to look down upon the reader. Better yet, he's seeking complicity. Some will say it's a common cliché, but that's exactly the point. Where else can we find a common space? Where?

With a name that resembles a cross between a corner bar and a racehorse, *Lil' Luck* will establish trust between author and reader. Luck's a nice word, and interestingly enough, the diminutive doesn't detract from it. Quite the opposite. With the lil' it's open to all comers, just like happiness, which it can replace metaphorically. The notion of being carefree, which the expression conveys, will be pleasantly felt. The glimmer of irony that peeks through should in no way be construed as aggressive.

Do you or *Do we have a choice?* will be used in moderation. The banality of this bogus question is too obvious and might spark some degree of disdainful weariness in the reader.

It seemed important at the time will introduce a distance proper to historical accounts. "Everything's relative," the reader will say, shrugging his shoulders. Or, "our ancestors were such stupid pricks."

The choice is yours will be a humanistic affirmation in that it allows us to imagine a certain forbearance in human relations. It's really not a question of knowing if you do have a choice. In fact, it's not bloody likely. But in contrast with Do you / Do we have a choice? which implies no choice, the same phrase formulated in the affirmative will appear to be gentler and more tolerable.

Or:

8. *Have you had your breakfast yet?*

The use of a phrase such as this will introduce an element of mystery. Why am I being asked such a thing? Is this persiflage? A provocation? Why? Will the key to the puzzle be revealed at the end of the work?

Finally, the reader will be confronted by the following dictum:

9. *Life's a bitch.*

This shall be the author's motto. But, as some question this platitude even today, he will employ it sparingly.

ON HUMANITY

WOULD IT BE SO BAD if humanity were to disappear? Some would be delighted. They've been clamoring for its disappearance for many a moon. It would lead to the liberation of other species, and the Earth would finally be able to breathe after the catastrophes brought about by the thoughtless and murderous parasites that we are.

But the subject of this book is the world.

CLIMATE CHANGE

SEVERAL OF THE SCENARIOS for the end of the world I am thinking about using here are taken from secret United States Defense
Department reports on climate change, the digital world, and the
dangers of globalization. I'll copy sentences that appear there in
the conditional and put them in the past tense. It's a trick of the
trade. For example, *This, in turn, would lead to a 12% reduction
in the average weight of cattle* will become *This, in turn, led to a
12% reduction in the average weight of cattle.*

At times, I'll leave them as is, but have them come out of a
character's mouth. For example, *"It is quite plausible that over the
next ten years the proof of sudden and violent climate change will
become indisputable,"* said the Green Party candidate.

Or even, *"Several years after its launch, the Human Brain
Project, the ambitious research program that sought to model the
structure and function of the human brain, was the object of a
heretofore unprecedented cyberattack,"* said the Minister of Digital
Development.

It is possible that the events I'm going to tell you about didn't
happen until several years or decades later. I don't remember anymore. No matter. Astrophysicists agree: there's little chance in
the meantime of coming across a planet stupid enough to want
to welcome the potential survivors of the human race.

I will also make use of other reports and documents: *Global
Trends, Strategic Contexts through to 2025*, or *Mapping the Global
Future.* Their authors rarely agree with one another. This increases
the possibility that one of them is correct.

DATES

I will also cheat on the dates. I'll push them off by a few years. For example, *2020: skirmishes on the borders and in the interior of Bangladesh, India, and China during a massive migration toward Myanmar* will become *2022: skirmishes on the borders and in the interior of Bangladesh, India, and China during a massive migration toward Myanmar.* Or, *2020: after the wave of terrorist attacks perpetrated in France and the U.K., the risk of civil war was confirmed when deadly clashes broke out in Toulouse, Marseille, and Birmingham* will become *2021*, and so on.

This way my book will remain current even after the events.

PERNOD-RICARD

LET'S RETURN TO GASPARD. We met at a translation conference in Arles, a city in France, the country in which we both resided at the time. Both of us were outstanding translators. Excellence exists, even if it can only be recognized by fellow brothers in excellence. The mediocre ones will always be quick to criticize, out of frustration when their mediocrity is partial, out of ineptitude when it's absolute.

The problem is, this professional excellence invariably leads to what one might call difficulty making ends meet, but since this is freelance work as they say, the ends can pop up quite unexpectedly. Gigs on the side are a necessity. Gaspard supplemented his income by composing advertising slogans for a spirits company, Pernod-Ricard, which produced Pernod, Ricard, Pastis 51, Suze, Soho, Scrue, and so on. He was the author of several slogans that struck a chord with the public.

DRINK IN MODERATION BUT DRINK UP!
Drink Responsibly. Alcohol abuse is dangerous to your health.

RICARD, A FRIEND BOTH HEADY AND HEADSTRONG
Drink Responsibly. Alcohol abuse is dangerous to your health.

SUZE, THE TRUE SUZERAIN OF LIQUEURS
Drink Responsibly. Alcohol abuse is dangerous to your health.

SOHO, SO-O GOOD!
Drink Responsibly. Alcohol abuse is dangerous to your health.

THAT RICARD. . . SUCH A CARD!
Drink Responsibly. Alcohol abuse is dangerous to your health.

PERNOD? PER OUI, MON AMI!
Drink Responsibly. Alcohol abuse is dangerous to your health.

Some of his other suggestions had been rejected by the head of
marketing.

ONE'S GOOD, BUT TWO'S EVEN BETTER
Drink Responsibly. Alcohol abuse is dangerous to your health.

BABE, I WANNA SCRUE!
Drink Responsibly. Alcohol abuse is dangerous to your health.

Drink Responsibly. Alcohol abuse is dangerous to your health was
a disclaimer required by law for any advertisement. For want
of a new war on European soil, something had to be found to
distract the people, and nothing distracts the people better than
knowing they're in danger.

Later, Gaspard had become, completely by accident and only
for the span of eight months, advisor to the stupidest American
President in history. He had moved to the United States. He then
had returned to France with enough in the bank to keep up his
lifestyle for a good long while. This had happened at the very
beginning of the last century of the Christian era.

More prosaically, I on the other hand became a writer.
Consequently, my primary occupation consisted of organizing
what are referred to as writing workshops, during which I made
people who wished to obtain the status of creative believe that
it was within their reach.

ON BENEDICTINES

IN SHORT, I was a translator gone bad. Translators were serious and delicate individuals. The three or four hundred essential books of the fifty centuries of writing that preceded the end of the world were in their hands. It was no walk in the park. With each new generation of readers three to four hundred books needed to be re-translated. In a world filled with halfwits, it was no walk in the park to attempt—completely in vain, more-over—to preserve the difference between honorable and hideous, between sincere and sycophantic, between true and real.

Writers of my era were bubble-blowers. All the same, with their cock-and-bull stories and their piss-poor metaphors. Their amphigories were so crappy they'd frequently publish the same book three or four years later as something completely new. Changing the title was all it took.

Bubble-blowers. Workers on the production line of vacuity. Benedictines of insignificance. I know what I'm talking about. You bought my book? You made a mistake.

ON THE NOVEL

FOR A WHILE, Gaspard himself had also surrendered to the fashion reigning in France at the time, in which all young people of a certain social status imagined writing, one day or another, a novel, or several. He chose to write a science fiction novel. His hero was a ninety-two-year-old man who had found a way to travel among the inhabited planets without being noticed. Ever since uncharted islands and continents disappeared from the surface of the Earth, inhabited planets provided a possible *topos* for the genre.

In his descriptions of extraterrestrial societies, Gaspard shamelessly lifted from old volumes of the *Journal des Sçavans*, which he had inherited from his grandfather. To the erudite and appealingly outdated descriptions, he would add commentaries of his own invention. His hero was a twentieth-century man and saw things differently than his predecessors.

The story ended badly. The old man, who had become completely senile, got lost in the depths of space and couldn't find his way back to Earth. He was doomed to wander among the planets until the end of the universe, which in any case was fast approaching. As an afterword, Gaspard introduced a short reflection on the fact that even though there were a ton of dangers out there that grabbed the attention of his contemporaries, nobody gave a damn about the expansion of the universe.

Unorganized, heterogeneous, and chock-full of subtle ideas, the manuscript, entitled *Upside-down Worlds*, had absolutely no chance of being published. After having received eighteen replies in the form of scornful silence, Gaspard had 150 copies printed at his own expense. He had managed to unload thirty at a moribund bookstore in his neighborhood—free with the purchase of another book. The owner died before being able to reduce the stack. His successor turned the old bookstore into a video game store. The first combat video games, which had just appeared on the market, were selling like hotcakes. That the whole world was on the brink of becoming a vast battlefield didn't diminish in the slightest people's desire to wage war in their own homes.

Of the remaining 120 copies, Gaspard had handed out fifteen or so to family and friends, then had left the rest on the stone parapets along the Seine in Paris before the *bouquinistes* arrived. The *bouquinistes* were used-book sellers who each possessed an 8- by 0.75-meter space along the banks of the Seine. Their emblem consisted of a lizard and a sword. The first symbolized the *bouquinistes* scrutinizing the horizon for sunny days to sell their wares; the latter their profession, which three and a half centuries earlier had been accorded the right to bear arms.

Fictitious or innate, too insipid or too outrageous, reality is never directly literary. to palm off his stuff needed to create an artificial reality, as fake as it was plausible, without transcendence or morality, while avoiding all and every stylistic pretention as far as possible.

Gaspard went back to his translations.

SOAKING TUBS

WE SPENT SEVERAL EVENINGS together in Arles before returning to Paris where Gaspard lived in a small one-bedroom apartment near the Bastille—a living/dining room, a bedroom, and a bathroom with a compact soaking tub and toilet. It was the soaking tub that fostered our mutual trust. I had one in my home, too. Soaking tubs had become rare. Most people who lived in small apartments preferred showers, more economical they said, both in terms of water and time. And, most importantly, more invigorating, and consequently, more dynamic and more modern. Most people wished to be dynamic and modern. It seemed important at the time.

I can no longer remember how we got onto the subject of bathrooms, soaking tubs, and showers, but nonetheless that's what helped us bond. We shared the same experience of living in small spaces—the compact soaking tub being the symbolic expression of a tub apartment—and the same aversion for showers and modernity. Modernity, how lugubrious. For life to preserve the illusion of some type of meaning, we have a duty to ourselves to live intemporally. Remaining outside of their time is the comic drama of people endowed with a modicum of common sense.

JAMMING

BEFORE LAYING INTO SODOM, Gomorrah, Admah, and Zeboim, God had cut his teeth by destroying what would have been humanity's first skyscraper, to be constructed in a place by the name of Babel. God didn't like the idea that people could work in concert and live together in a vertical city.

The means of destruction was less spectacular but all the more wicked. God invented some sort of jamming device. For History's first skyscraper, the first technological feat. He placed the device at the foot of the skyscraper under construction and set it off. The following day, the workers didn't get what they told each other, both literally and figuratively. One would ask for bricks and he would get a trowel. When another asked for the ropes to be hoisted, they would be lowered. The bell was rung, it sounded hollow. All this ended up cracking people's spirits. People went off in separate directions. They forgot their language and had to invent others.

That's how Gaspard and I became translators.

WESTERN SOCIETY

THE SOCIETY OF WHICH we were part was called *Western*. It was the most extraordinary society of the last two millennia. It invented linear time, brotherly love, senior citizens, nuclear fission, ecology and veganism, the future and the past. It had developed concepts demonstrating that it was not terribly important to know where we came from and others demonstrating the importance of our origins. It had sent all kinds of objects out of Earth's atmosphere. It had discovered that the Universe was like an onion and that it was possible to peel it all the way to the bud, which was called the *Big Bang*. It had calculated its age:

$$\frac{\Omega}{2} = q_0 + \frac{\Lambda c^2}{3H^2}$$

It had discovered the interdependence of free markets and free love. It had imagined the ubiquity of God, and then His absence. It had invented surveillance cameras, the common good, genomic sequencing, and preventative war.

DANGERS

BUT BY THE BEGINNING of the twenty-first century, a gnaw-
ing worry had begun to grip Western society. Multiple dangers
seemed to call this so beautifully crafted society into question.
Persistent social inequality, international institutions in crisis,
increasing energy needs, cyber warfare, intensifying external conflicts, omnipresent insecurity, rapes, pandemics, massacres, ston-
ings, beheadings—the choice is yours. Several important international summits to defend against these threats had taken place.
Yes! It was possible! It was urgent, and the task important. The
world needed to be refashioned, and quick. Make people's understanding of emerging global risks evolve and consolidate the
management thereof. Define sustainable competition, promote
equitable and inclusive growth, improve global governance, and
restore confidence to younger generations.

The future of the world depended on it.

AH!

AH! *THE FUTURE*, such a tricky word. In old French there was the expression *to leave the future.*

"Sir! Are you leaving the future?"

"Aye, milady. 'Twould be difficult for me to dwell there another second."

THE AGE OF THE UNIVERSE

THE VARIOUS RESEARCH PROJECTS conducted to determine the age of the universe produced similar results, and they speak volumes. The galaxies and stars were moving away from Earth at a faster and faster rate. The entire Universe was fleeing the human race. No friends, no kindred spirits in the cosmos, not one single extraterrestrial scientist crazy enough to want to study life on Earth.

CATASTROPHIES

THE END OF THE WORLD had been predicted numerous times over the course of human history. During the twentieth and twenty-first centuries it ought to have occurred forty-two times.

That each of these times didn't come to pass, or at least not completely, by no means obviates the next. Quite the opposite: statistically speaking, with each failure the odds increase considerably. Ends of the world are like human births. A woman's gestative capacity is only one in four. The three prior copulations are both necessary and fruitless.

The reasons for the end of the world were varied. The fury of a disappointed God raining down on humanity and exterminating it once and for all. The planet colliding with a near-Earth asteroid. A meteorite shower falling on Earth and causing a deadly tsunami. Asteroid collisions leading to melting polar caps. A mysterious event causing the South Pole to shift from its axis. The end of the calendar cycle leading to something terrible. Extraterrestrials armed with sophisticated weapons invading the Earth. An inversion of energy currents making the Earth pass into the fourth dimension. The Earth disappearing into a black hole created by the Large Hadron Collider. A sudden end to the magnetic field allowing solar winds to penetrate the atmosphere. The Earth's atmosphere suddenly blowing into space, and the oceans drying up. Have you had your breakfast yet?

According to an American think tank, there was only, both presently and symbolically, one minute until the end of the world. The organization brought together researchers who year after year entertained themselves by evaluating the more or less negligible chances of humanity's survival. When it was looking its best, at the beginning of the 1990s, humanity had seventeen minutes to live.

1948	*******
1949	***
1950	***
1951	***
1952	***
1953	**
1954	**
1955	**
1956	**
1957	**
1958	**
1959	**
1960	******
1961	******
1962	***
1963	************
1964	************
1965	************
1966	************
1967	************
1968	*******
1969	**********
1970	**********
1971	**********
1972	************
1973	************
1974	*********
1975	*********
1976	*********
1977	*********
1978	*********
1979	*********

1980	*******
1981	****
1982	****
1983	***
1984	****
1985	***
1986	***
1987	***
1988	******
1989	******
1990	**********
1991	******************
1992	*****************
1993	*****************
1994	*****************
1995	**************
1996	*************
1997	*************
1998	*********
1999	*********
2000	*********
2001	*********
2002	*******
2003	*******
2004	*******
2005	*******
2006	*******
2007	*****
2008	*****
2009	*****
2010	******
2011	******
2012	*****
2013	*****
2014	****
2015	***
2016	**

2017   **
2018   **
2019   *

The researchers justified their prediction of "*extraordinary and undeniable threats*" stating it was due to "*unchecked climate change, global nuclear weapons modernizations, and outsized nuclear weapons arsenals.*"

They forgot, please see above, the wrath of God, who is always liable to try out new methods.

GODS AND GENERALS

LOT'S WIFE had turned around to see the first bombing in human history. God didn't like that. If she talks, people will like me less, he said to himself. This lesson was kept in mind later during the bombings of civilian populations in the twentieth century. The bombings of London, Dresden, or Hué were designed to sow fear among the population, but were not presented as such. Reasons like the need to destroy enemy infrastructure, enemy headquarters and railway stations, or factories producing regulation footwear for enemy soldiers were discussed. In short, everything generals dream of during times of peace. The population just happened to be there through an unfortunate series of events.

If we admit we kill civilians in order to terrify other civilians, the generals had told themselves, people will like us less.

MUSLIM ANGELS

THE STORY OF LOT and his wife is also told in the holy book of the Muslims. Here, however, Lot's wife was condemned even before the bombing. The Muslim angels made it clear from the start. They said: "We'll save Lot's family, except his wife." Muslim angels were wiser than Jewish angels. They knew the end of the story. Might as well save time.

GENERAL WRIGHT

GASPARD'S FATHER, Pierre-Maurice Victor Émiel, was born on 11 May 1919, six months to the day after the signing of the armistice which marked the end of the Great War, also called *The War to End All Wars*. The ceasefire, which was signed at five o'clock in the morning, was to go into effect at eleven. Towards eight thirty General Wright of the 89th American infantry division decided to attack an enemy-occupied village so that his troops could take baths and therefore celebrate the newly found peace in a dignified manner. The attack caused the deaths of 298 infantry, but the survivors were able to avail themselves of the village's three fountains as well as the kindness of its last remaining inhabitants.

Pierre-Maurice's mother, Augustine Joséphine Louise Victorine Buchon, farm girl and single mother, was married eighteen months later to a merchant in Béthune, Jean-Baptiste Justin Léopold Boisvert, fifteen years her senior. He dearly loved his adopted son, taught him how to fashion reed pipes, and made sure his childhood was peaceful.

Which didn't prevent the adopted child from being called a Kraut by his classmates, who were better informed than he was about his dubious origins.

The word *Kraut* was an offensive slur for Germans. It was against the Krauts that General Wright had ordered the charge.

The Boisverts would not have any children. Jean-Baptiste was felled by choroidal melanoma in 1936, at the age of sixty.

Augustine passed away nineteen years later from Laennec's cirrhosis. General Wright had certainly been dead for a while.

So it goes.

ALLIED COUNTRIES

IF GERMANY HAD WON the previous war, the next one would not have taken place. The sixty million dead would have lived their lives. Some of them would never have heard of war. Others would have scraped by, living in peace under German occupation, Austrian administration, or Turkish rule. Others would have experienced less deadly wars in which they would have lost at most an eye or a leg.

But in 1939 a new war broke out, one that made Adolf the Kraut famous. Pierre-Maurice, conscripted into the fifty-fifth Infantry Division in Soissons, fought for several months near Forbach, a city on the German border and then in Stonne, a town farther north, which was taken and retaken seventeen times by the French army and eighteen times by the German army. Pierre-Maurice was taken prisoner and spent the rest of the war in a Stalag in western Pomerania, in eastern Germany. *Stalag* was an abbreviation for *Stammlager*, and indicated a camp for non-commissioned personnel. Officers were interned in *Oflags*, an abbreviation for *Offizierlager*.

His five years of captivity were followed by four months of walking westward through bleak countryside and villages destroyed by Allied bombings. Allied airplanes would occasionally bomb the column of prisoners, believing they were Germans. German citizens were also fleeing to the west, hoping to escape the Russians, who were arriving from the east. Several years before, the Germans and Russians had been allied against the Polish. Then the Germans invaded Russia, and the Russians and the Allies became allies. Later, after the Russian and Allied victory over Germany, the Russians and the Poles in turn became allies against the Allies.

THE FIRST MAN

ADOLF HITLER didn't like Jews. Jews were descendants of an ancient people, the Hebrews, who had discovered that their god was the one god. Then, in order to find an explanation for the evil of men and the inanity of human life, they worked out the theory of a sin committed by the first man on Earth and of which all humans were guilty at birth. Newborns, seeing themselves punished for the sin of some guy they'd never heard of, soon became tetchy and quarrelsome. Growing up they committed all kinds of sins, their corruption being innate. A vicious circle that would bring delight only to depraved philosophers.

The god of the Hebrews did promise to send them, sooner or later, a Savior who would put an end to this absurd system. But while waiting for this to happen various catastrophes struck the Hebrews, such that they found themselves scattered across the world, and became Jews. Adolf suspected them of wanting to corrupt humanity in their image.

THE LOIMA HILLS

GASPARD'S MOTHER, Mrs. Hélène Boisvert, née Verech, born on 16 October 1925, the day of the signing of what are called the Locarno Treaties, which guaranteed the borders of Germany and thus the collective security of Europe—was from a secular Jewish family of Ukrainian-Polish origins. Her grandfather was Haim Verechov, a fellow traveler of Theodor Herzl, the late-nineteenth-century theoretician of Zionism. Zionism was a political movement whose aim was to establish a Jewish State. According to family lore, it was in fact Haim who, at the 1903 Zionist Congress in Basel, had discreetly suggested to Herzl that he conclude his speech with a quotation from Psalm 137 of the holy book of the Jews: "If I forget thee, O Jerusalem, let my right hand forget her cunning! Shalom! Shalom!"

Jerusalem was the city that, whilom, the invisible god of the Jews inhabited.

Shalom was a Hebrew word that meant well-being, peace, hello, and goodbye. According to erudite Jews, it was also one of the names of the one god. Furthermore, it was forbidden to say hello in unclean places, bathrooms, and latrines.

Haim Verechov was also the author of a utopian novel, *Eine Reise nach Freiland*, which was published under a pen name in 1893. The story took place in Africa, in the territory that would later become Kenya. At the time it was a nameless country that the Massai, Kikuyu, Somali, Oromo, Swahili, Sirikwa, Boran, Samburu, and several others shared. The whole coterie had been merrily waging war against one another for the last five thousand years. An ideal place, according to Gaspard's great-grandfather, in which to found a free and egalitarian Jewish state, where all men would enjoy the right to a decent life.

As a result of the novel's publication, ten years later Hertzel himself named Haim a member of a commission charged with studying the possibility of establishing a provisional Jewish state under British protectorate in Uganda, a country inhabited by the Toro, Ankole, Karagwe, Ganda, Baganda, and several other tribes. This was the idea of the British Secretary of State for the Colonies, Joseph Chamberlain, the man who invented concentration camps in South Africa. His son Arthur would become Prime Minister and would later distinguish himself in particular for signing, in a German town by the name of Munich, the agreement with Adolf the Kraut that became famous for having facilitated the greatest massacre in the history of humanity, except for the one that would take place on the occasion of the end of the world.

The members of the commission returned from Uganda horrified. With protectorates and insurrections come rivers of blood, which flowed day after day from the high plains. And that was without mentioning the British grunts, with their fish-like expressions, who treated them like sub-humans. But without malice nonetheless.

At the time, the British had a reputation for having fish eyes and being the stupidest nation in the world. Now that was a decisive advantage. It isn't intelligence that allows nations to progress. Other countries will later have the opportunity to confirm this, albeit only briefly.

Haim had contracted poliomyelitis and died there. His body was not repatriated. It rests in the Loima Hills. One of many siblings, he himself fathered but a single rug rat. He was seven and was Gaspard's maternal grandfather.

THE CROWD

WHEN HE RETURNED from Munich, the crowd waiting to thank Arthur Chamberlain for having the expertise necessary to face the menace of war and save democracy was waving hats and scarves. Arthur exited the airplane and declared, "I am bringing peace to my country for generations."

A JEWISH JOKE

HÉLÈNE VERECH was baptized at the age of twelve in the name of the Father, the Son, and the Holy Spirit. The baptism took place just a few short weeks after the promulgation of anti-Jewish laws in Germany. Her parents had foresight.

Which reminds me of a joke. A German Jew, arriving in France in 1938 and newly naturalized, asks to have his last name changed. No problem, says the civil servant. What's your name? Katzmann, says the Jew. Let's see, says the civil servant. *Katz*, okay, that's German for *sha*. And *Mann*, in French that's *lom*. Alright, we'll call you Shalom!

That's a Jewish joke.

Hélène Verech later received a Christian education and became enough of a believer that she would pray, from time to time, to the Mother of the Son, asking for Her benevolence and protection.

ON DEMOCRACIES

By bringing peace to Great Britain, Arthur was toiling for democracy. The former allowed the latter to flourish. This too was a Western discovery. It was a practical term. Even though it was weighed down by an overabundance of meanings and condemned by philologists and killjoys from time to time, most politicians valued it. There were all kinds of democracies: liberal, Christian, Marxist, young, direct, indirect, semi-direct, citizen, participatory, representative, parliamentary, popular, unpopular, market, incomplete, developing, failing.

At the time of the Munich Agreement, the word referred not only to a system of political organization, but also to a kind of system for social relationships.

Democracy was recognized by the fact that its citizens were of the opinion that they could weigh in on the evolution of society and that they agreed with each other only very seldom, and therein it differed from authoritarian regimes, whose citizens didn't feel that they could weigh in on anything and agreed on almost everything.

But little by little people in democracies started to think the same things, albeit democratically. So the only difference from totalitarian regimes was that individuals remained convinced that these were their own unique ideas, their own authentic opinions. From time to time they would denounce attacks on freedom of thought in non-democratic countries, all the while oblivious to the fact that they had lost the ability to forge free thoughts many moons ago, assuming they had ever possessed it.

Be that as it may, authoritarian regimes mocked democracies by pointing out their inability to offer their citizens visionary and sweeping policies.

IT'S NOT A BARREL OF FUN

"Democracy is the most moronic regime."

"Oh?"

"Democracy is the desire to please the most people. Am I wrong?"

"Technically no."

"Most people, by far, are morons. Am I wrong?"

"Probably not."

"Tomorrow, just like today, most people will be morons. Am I wrong?"

"I hope so."

"All that morons want is to have enough money to buy themselves a big screen so they can watch moronic shows and tell other morons their opinions the next day. There are also some who'd rather play moronic games, either by themselves or with other morons. Am I wrong?"

"You're exaggerating."

"All morons want is to earn enough money to replace their living room couch or buy a bigger house and have someone to mate with in order to prove they're still living. Am I wrong?"

"That's human nature."

"That's what I've been telling you. It's human nature. Morons are more human than non-morons."

"Still, you're pushing it a bit far."

"There are wimpy morons— the ones who dream of couches and houses— and then there are bloodthirsty morons, who don't have an ounce of democratic feeling, who kill wimpy morons."

"I'd say it's better to be a wimpy moron than a bloodthirsty moron."

"Except wimpy morons aren't willing to die to defend their couches."

"That's also a good thing."

"Except they die anyway."

"That happens to everybody."

"Now they do still have one thing in common. I mean the wimps and the bloodthirsty ones."

"Oh, really?"

"They believe that the universe was created as a backdrop to their moronic lives."

"As a backdrop, that's totally . . ."

"For us, democracy is the backdrop."

"Exactly. Still, there's worse."

"That Englishman. The one who replaced Arthur. After Munich."

"Winston?"

"He said that democracy was the worst form of government."

"Which fits with what you were saying."

"So far, yes. But then he immediately added, except for all the others."

"I see."

"It's all quite sad."

"Let's just say it's not a barrel of fun."

ADOLF'S TALENT

ADOLF WAS BORN in a small Austrian town named Braunau am Inn on 20 April 1889, the day of the ninety-seventh anniversary of Prussia's declaration of war on France. According to neighbors' accounts, his mother was a modest, pious woman who divided her time between church, household chores, and the education of her children. She had brown hair and blue-gray eyes. His father, a customs inspector, was an authoritarian husband and a stickler for discipline. He beat his wife on average once a week, as was customary at the time.

The young Adolf would have liked to become a painter. He had real talent, a school teacher said of him. But he had failed the admissions test for the Academy of Fine Arts in Vienna, the capital of the country. *"Awkward lines. Muddled composition. Conventional imagination."* That's what the Academy of Fine Arts had declared.

Soon afterward, Adolf discovered another talent: a persuasive power over those around him. A skillful orator and excellent pedagogue, he rapidly managed to found a pugnacious political party, win elections, become the most popular politician in the country, and launch a world war.

THE ONE WHO DIGS

ADOLF SHOULDN'T have been named Hitler, which comes from *Hiedl*, an underground spring. His father's name was Alois Schicklgruber, a surname that means the One-who-digs-the-ditch-to-drain-the-liquid-manure. Alois was the bastard son of Maria Anna Schicklgruber. She later married and changed her last name upon the request of Alois's step-uncle who wished to make him his legatee. In short, Adolf should have been named the One-who-digs-the-ditch-to-drain-the-liquid-manure. And, in spite of all of his oratorical skills, no reasonable person in the crowd would have yelled, "Long live the One-who-digs-the-ditch-to-drain-the-liquid-manure!" With a name like that, Adolf would at best have become a customs inspector and the most horrendous of wars would never have taken place.

But still. If he had found in his entourage a shrewd propagandist or some marketing director, he could have recast it as a good old bloodletting—the ditch transformed into a rivulet and the manure into the blood of all those who sullied the German race: Jews, murderers, thieves, cripples, degenerates, the insane. Then the crowd would have yelled, "Long live the Bleeder of the Nation!"

ON THE FIRST NAME

HITLER'S FIRST NAME refers to the Greek *adelphos*, which means *brother*. The word was formed from the prefix *a-* and the noun *delphus*, which means *womb*. The prefix *a-* coupled with womb was a copulative prefix.

Delphus also gave birth to the city of Delphi, which was previously home to the temple of the oracle, as well as to the dolphin, a sea creature, which, in days of yore, liked to wiggle in front of people.

ON THE CHRISTIAN RELIGION

AMONG THE 9,015 FAITHS recorded in the world at the dawn of the last millennium, the Christian faith came in first with 33.06% of believers.

Believers were people who feared one or several gods and endeavored to mollify them through their actions and prayers.

Originally, Christians were a dissident Jewish sect. They used the Jewish religion to proclaim a single god, while designating to him a Son, which the Father is reported to have had with the assistance of a Spirit and a young virgin who didn't suspect a thing before an angel came to apprise her of the situation. Christians upheld the idea that the Son was the long-awaited Savior. His name was Jesus.

Jews represented 0.23% and Muslims 20.28% of the fearers. At the dawn of the last millennium, they were the ones causing problems. Their god was called Allah.

MORALITY

THE NUMBER OF VICTIMS of the bombing of Dresden in comparison to Hiroshima demonstrated the usefulness of conventional weapons. Not subject to non-proliferation treaties, they remained a valuable asset as long as one knew the right conditions under which to use them.

Bombings could be directed against enemy populations in two different ways. Either by immediately identifying them as the objective or by targeting warehouses filled with explosives located in densely populated areas. That way it was the enemy's own means of destruction that would kill the enemies. It might be possible to discern something like an effluvium of morality here.

It was also possible to take possession of enemy equipment that did not theoretically have a specific war-related function and transform it into a guided missile. That's what the Muslim god-fearers managed to do at the beginning of the twenty-first century.

GOD IS GREAT

WHILE THE NINETEENTH CENTURY had started eleven years early and the twentieth fourteen years late, the twenty-first had started more or less on time, with a lag of barely nine months.

A common element of the three was that they were followed by wars here and there, which caused other wars, then still other wars, which all ended up melding into one. They saw the appearance of new strategies, amazing new weapons, and daring innovations. Likewise, the Muslim god-fearers had imagined a new bombing technique using airliners.

The Muslim god-fearers were waging war against those who feared another god as much as against the non-fearers or even those who in the past had feared a god but who had stopped fearing him for various reasons—all of these, generally speaking, were quite valid from the standpoint of basic logic.

They were also waging war against other Muslim god-fearers who feared the same god, just not enough.

They were thus operating in two arenas, which had alrady been exploited several centuries earlier by Christian god-fearers: one during the crusades, the other during the wars of religion.

Either the Christians were early or the Muslims late. Since the idea of time is an invention, no one's ever on time.

During the massacres the Muslim god-fearers proclaimed *God is merciful*, while the massacred cried out *Oh my God!*

"Ladies and gentlemen: here the captain. Please sit down keep remaining seating."

"In the name of God, the all merciful, the very merciful."

"No, no."

"Shut up."

"Oh my God."

"In the name of God. In the name of God. I bear witness that there is no other God than God."

"Come on guys. God is the greatest. God is the greatest. Oh guys. God is the greatest."

"Huh?"

"What?"

"Oh God. Oh the very merciful."

"What?"

"Trust in God."

"What?"

"Pull it down."

"Oh my God."

"God is the greatest."

"God is the greatest."

"God is the greatest."

"God is the greatest."

ON HEROISM

DYING STUPIDLY is not an answer. I read that sentence long ago in a book. It was an adventure story about bandits and brigands. The story took place during the good old days of the wars of religion. The person to whom the adage was addressed was named Martin. Armed with a simple bludgeon, he was getting ready to lunge at a horde of bandits who were armed to the teeth and holding captive his beloved. By saying this his interlocutor wished him to understand that not only would he not rescue her but moreover he would get himself killed in the act. But on second thought, this line is surprising. It assumes the possibility of dying intelligently. And furthermore that dying intelligently can produce the *answer*. How does one die intelligently? In Martin's case, by obtaining his immediate goal, namely to die while rescuing his beloved from the bandits' clutches. More generally, by fulfilling one's destiny, divine will, one's assigned mission: normally it involves killing others. The death of some brings joy to others, a bit like inheritances. But as it so happens, killing bandits, crucifying false prophets, gassing Jews, scalping invaders, guillotining malcontents is not in and of itself enough. Death must follow to achieve the desired answer—dying after having killed a large number of people, giving one's life while taking others'. Who cares in the end if they died in the stupidest way possible. This is not an executioner standing before his victims; before his victims stands a hero. Dying heroically by blanketing yourself with explosives and taking a stroll at the Sunday market—that's the answer. And bam! No more stomach, no more butt, no more balls, just a couple of bits and fresh meat all around.

Martin, with his silly bludgeon, certainly would not have fit the bill.

THE JOKE ABOUT THE TWO CHINESE

Do you know the joke about the two Chinese? A gentleman who is not Chinese, accompanied by a woman who is no more Chinese than he is, walks into a café and asks the waiter, "Two Chinese, please." The waiter responds, "I'll need to check with my manager about that."

I'll tell you the rest later.

ON THE SURNAME MARTIN

IT JUST SO HAPPENED that Martin was the most common surname in France. Their patron saint, Saint Martin, was renowned for being a kind soul. One winter's eve, he shared his cloak with an unknown man who turned out to be the Son of God, descended from heaven in search of humaneness. In remembrance of his kind act, his name was given to children who were abandoned on church steps, in front of public assistance buildings, or, in my time, in boxes specifically designed for this purpose.

Martins were everywhere, even more numerous than Jews.

A SIMPLER WORLD

MARTIN WAS ALSO THE NAME I would give when asked, and what's the name for the reservation? Everyone in France could write Martin. We should have somehow made it so that everyone could recall all the names in the world. The world would have been simpler, more open, more communicative, more direct, more sincere, more friendly.

"What's your first name?"

"Martin."

"And your last name?"

"Martin."

"Whoa, dude!"

In short, it was better to be named Martin than Ouředník. And yet! If I had been born in Madagascar, my name might have been Andriraoantsitambintsana. And what's the name? Andriraoantsitambintsana!

ON THE NAME GASPARD

THERE WERE THREE KINGS who visited Jesus, the future Savior of Humanity. One of them bore the name Gaspard. They had had the revelation that a child prodigy, king of the heavens, would be born in a stable near Bethlehem, a Jewish hamlet.

Gaspard bowed respectfully before the newborn, but did not kneel, for he too was a king. He did not cross himself, nor did he make the sign of the cross on the infant's forehead, for the cross had not yet become the symbol of redemption, the remission of sins, and eternal life through God. People didn't yet cross their fingers when spouting lies to annul the action by which they had just contravened divine proscriptions. People didn't yet play hopscotch in the shape of a cross to reach the semicircle of heaven at the top.

In order to redeem mankind, Jesus, son of God, obeying God the father, allowed himself to be crucified. Ever since, the world has been headed for annihilation. The Christian religion had foreseen its own failure. The Savior, who during his lifetime had a marked penchant for convoluted parables, was definitely asking too much of fallen humanity. It just couldn't work.

From redemption to Apocalypse, the cards were dealt.

ON BOOKS

THE PRIMARY PURPOSE of books is to avert collective suicide. They have a social role. Now it may happen that someone will commit suicide after having read a book. That's an accident. The majority of readers don't commit suicide because they know their desire for abnegation is shared by all sensible readers. It comforts them and at the same time engenders a feeling of solidarity. I can't do that to them, to my companions in misfortune, to my brothers in misery.

ON WRITERS

THE MORE WRITERS there are, the more the exasperation. Either they're bad—their incompetence afflicts us—or they're good—what they say overwhelms us.

QUITE RIGHT

"Seventy years without a war. That's not normal."
"You think?"
"It's unheard of."
"Everything has a beginning."
"Quite right. And an end, too."

INCESTOUS RELATIONS

ONCE THEY HAD ESCAPED the bombings, Lot's daughters discreetly slept with their alcoholic father in order to ensure the perpetuation of the human race. It seemed important at the time. What's more, sleeping with one's parents was considered almost normal then. It was only later that scientists discovered this could have psychological side effects and even produce mental deficiencies in the descendants.

The first incestuous roll in the hay of Western history occurred between a murderer by the name of Cain and his mother. This relationship brought into the world a daughter who would become the wife of her father. Cain's mother then would have another son with the father of her son who would then sleep with his mother. His name would be Seth, and he would have a son with his mother by the name of Enos. The child that Cain would have with his daughter would be named Enoch. The children that Lot's daughters would have with their father would be named Moab and Ammom.

Lot, drunk as a skunk at the time in question, and seeing his daughters packing on the pounds, fruitlessly wondered who could have gotten them pregnant. His daughters didn't let out a peep. Girly secrets.

ON THE FAMILY

INCESTUOUS RELATIONSHIPS seemed to be the key to social success. Adolf the Kraut's paternal grandfather, for example, a certain Johann Nepomuk, was also his maternal great grandfather. When all's well with the family, all's well.

But at the time when Gaspard and I were living, that is, just before the end of the world, the Western family had lost its luster. Incestuous relationships were rare. So were children. Men's sperm more frequently ended up in women's mouths than in their vaginas. That's one of the reasons people started talking about a postmodern society. A postmodern society was a society in which historical rationality had become fuzzy and beliefs inherited from the previous generation even fuzzier. Ergo, what's the point in producing offspring?

An evolution related to the loss of cultural identity, said some, a process that heralds any decline worth its name, flaccid and irreversible.

PROPHECY

WHOEVER SHALL ENTER THE TEMPLE
WILL MEET MERCHANTS;
THE FIELDS WILL EMPTY;
THE BARBARIANS WILL ENTER THE CITIES;
THE ILLUSION MONGERS
WILL PEDDLE THEIR POISON;
MAN WILL HAVE CHANGED
THE FACE OF THE LAND;
HATRED WILL SPREAD
LIKE FIRE IN A FOREST;
THE BARBARIANS
WILL MASSACRE SOLDIERS;
PEOPLE WILL SLIT EACH OTHER'S THROATS;
SAVAGERY WILL REIGN ON EARTH;
LIFE WILL BECOME
A DAILY APOCALYPSE.

The prophecy of Jean of Jerusalem was a big fat fake. Discovered, according to the preface of the published manuscript, in the archives of the monastery of Trzebnica, Poland, in 1927, it was reportedly composed in 1099 by a certain Jean de Vézelay, known as Jean of Jerusalem, who was supposedly one of the founders of the Order of the Knight Templars, an order with a monastic-military calling. This calling was contradictory only in appearance; they would eviscerate Muslims while making war more pious. The Knights Templar lived parsimoniously—they had the right to only two shirts and two sets of breeches, fasted four times per week, and shared an *écuelle* between two. After several decades they had amassed enough wealth to become the richest bankers in Europe.

They would have made excellent Americans. People succeed so much more when they start from nothing!

The scads of inconsistencies between the text and the mindset of the era should have been blindingly obvious to anyone, assuming the person knew how to read. To offer but this outrageous line as an example: *life will become a daily apocalypse.* For eleventh-century knights, the apocalypse was a unique, non-repeatable event. It was, moreover, a happy ending.

In spite of this, scholars, both diplomaed and self-proclaimed, took a good dozen years finally and painfully to arrive at this conclusion: the prophecy of Jean of Jerusalem is a big fat fake.

But like most fakes it proved to be astonishingly correct.

People then started actively to seek the forger. For a while Gaspard's maternal grandfather, Jacob Verechov, the one who had the good idea of making his daughter a Christian and sending her to France, was the prime suspect. At the time he was a professor of philology at the University of Gdansk, a Polish city with a majority German population.

But Jacob was too cultured to talk about daily apocalypses or, in a text supposedly written by an unlettered knight during the Middle Ages, to refer to Cassandra or Laocoön, prophets of antiquity.

That, incidentally, is what led to his downfall. When the time came his neighbors denounced him as a Jew. They found him too learned to be honest, too aloof to be frank.

ON THE LIVES OF PROPHETS

CASSANDRA AND LAOCOÖN were true prophets. Anticipating the monstrosities that humanity was preparing to inflict, they endeavored to warn their contemporaries in bygone Anatolia.

Cassandra was a young woman of great beauty with whom a god, by the name of Apollo, fell in love. He insisted that she sleep with him. In this bygone world, before the coming of the Savior, gods slept with women and goddesses with men, occasionally begetting demi-gods, who in turn begat quarter-gods, and so on, which was a bit like in mixed-race colonies where the members of the population were classified according to their degree of blood kinship with the original white person—mulattos, quadroons, octoroons, capres, and griffes.

His balls starting to turn blue, Apollo proposed to give Cassandra the gift of prophecy in exchange for future romps. Cassandra appeared to accept, but after becoming a prophet, dropped him like a bad habit. Now, since he couldn't take back what he'd given her, Apollo spat in her mouth so that no one would ever believe her predictions.

It was awful. In vain did she alert her pregnant mother that her unborn child would bring about the fall of the empire. In vain did she warn the defenders of her home town about the silly ruses of the besieging troops. In vain did she make her lover aware of the danger he was facing. The more she burrowed through time the crazier she appeared. The more she insisted, the more she was shunned. She was murdered, with no regrets.

Laocoön lived at the same time and met the fate of someone

who can see but who can't be understood. He too had attempted to come to the aid of his contemporaries by sharing his lugubrious visions. They jeered at him.

Over the entire course of human history prophets and augurs have been mistreated by the idiots they've tried to forewarn. Every time they foretold an imminent disaster, people laughed in their faces. Then, once disaster struck, people accused them of being the cause. Likewise, in my time, in my squeaky-clean era the term *self-fulfilling prophecy* was invented—a coinage idiots employ to disburden themselves of their own cowardice.

"It's your own fault because you predicted it!"

GASPARD BECOMES AN ADVISOR

I DIDN'T FIND MUCH in Gaspard's notebooks about why an obscure French translator was hired to be part of the American President's team of advisors. *"Contacted by some guy from the Secretary of State's Office who wants to see me 'related to a matter concerning me.' When are these wankers ever going to learn to speak?"* Then, the day after the meeting, *"Box of Matches wants me to come back to the States. The President's niece! Advisor! And I don't even have a suit!"*

Nothing else, or almost. I have to imagine the situation based solely on Gaspard's opinion of the President once he was there.

The day after his election, eager to show his originality straightaway, the democratically elected and stupidest President in the country's history voiced the desire to include a European on his team of advisors. Find me a European who speaks good English, he said to his Chief of Staff. But not a politician, okay? A guy who's got some culture. Who reads books. A member of society. I mean civil. You know, a European. But not some English dude, okay? Fed up with the English. Not a German either. Bunch of namby-pamby pacifists. First, they cram two fucking world wars down our throats, then they start screaming as soon as we want to base some missiles in their country. No Jews, okay? That's bad luck. Maybe a Polack. Or a Norwegian. No, not a Norwegian, that's not eco-friendly. Hey, a French guy. They're funny. Find me some French guy who speaks good English. There's gotta be one out there somewhere.

The Chief of Staff was slowly descending the stairs wondering

81

which deputy director he was going to palm this off on when he found himself nose to nose with the President's niece. Her name was Mary. She was known for slipping French words into her sentences like, *voilà, zut, à la vôtre, à la bonne heure*, that kind of stuff. It irritated the presidential campaign staff, but charmed her uncle.

The Chief of Staff saw this as a sign from the Almighty and approached her.

Back when Gaspard knew her, she was called Box of Matches or even Book of Matches, BOM, BOM. Stumpy legs, wide shoulders, nearly nonexistent neck, protruding knee caps. Gaspard had slept with her three or four times out of politeness. At the time women slept with toads out of kindness, and men with dogs out of gallantry. As an homage to the fairer sex, gallantry included the homely. So it was in the old world.

She was grateful to him for it. Old affairs of the heart leave lasting memories.

"Sure, Gaspard, *voilà!* Oh, but *zut*, where is he now. . . I haven't got the foggiest. I hope he's doing okay."

The Chief of Staff then directed his colleagues to call the State Department to inquire about a Frenchman, about fifty years old, who had lived in the United States in the eighties, and who answered to the name of Gaspard. Once in possession of his complete identification information, he called the French ambassador personally. The rest was child's play. Thinking that one day he'd be able to translate only those authors whom he believed merited it, Gaspard accepted, primarily lured by the potential gain. The proposed salary well surpassed everything he'd ever earned before. Plus he was curious. He did request, however, a two-month delay so that he could finish the translation of a previously unpublished work by Leslie Marmon Silko. He was a man of another era.

GASPARD AT THE WHITE HOUSE

THE FACE AND SKULL of the President would have delighted the physiognomists of centuries past. Flat brow: mediocrity, lack of imagination. Close set and thin eyebrows: moral deficiencies. Deep-set eyes: taste for intrigue. Thin lips: cupidity. Saggy cheeks: masturbatory tendencies. Fleshy chin: quarrelsome.

The whole topped off with blue eyes and the honest look of an experienced liar.

Agile, he had that spring in his step favored by ambitious Americans who plan on remaining flexible and active until the final throes of death.

If we are to believe Gaspard's notes, the President really liked him. He really liked listening to him pontificate on the policies that the United States should pursue in order to improve the world someday. He really liked hearing him cite American authors he'd never heard of. He really liked his accent, which was thick enough to cut through camembert. He dragged him around everywhere with him, much to the chagrin of his indigenous advisors. He called him "my little Frenchie," "my intellectual," "my Parisian from Stinky-Cheese-upon-Beretville," and "my transatlantic frog." Then, after the President learned during a dinner with the Italian ambassador of the existence of a European country way far out in Europe, "my Albanian."

Gaspard accepted all this willingly based on a belief he held: stupidity, all things considered, was more fascinating than intelligence, which by definition was limited.

Box of Matches had presented Gaspard as a distinguished

political journalist who published in prestigious journals under various pseudonyms and who had connections in the most elite of political circles. Even before Gaspard's arrival the President's men quickly discovered the ruse, but the President had decided to hire him nonetheless, as a kind of court jester. His official duties were to compile summaries of the French press and to write analyses, which no one read, on what the President called French political tendencies.

After arriving and appearing on television two or three times, Gaspard had become what Americans of a certain socio-economic status hated the most: a French caricature. He was still handsome and intelligent, two traits bearable in themselves, but insufferable when combined. Too elegant. Too nonchalant in the way he would sit down and cross his legs. A blazer casually draped across his shoulders put the final touch to the public's loathing.

French Frippery, read the newspaper headlines. Or: *A Frog-Eater on the Presidential Team.* Or: *Has the Semblance of Elegance Replaced Political Analysis?*

At the time, the American press was constantly rehashing the wars of religion, daily lambasting the French and the Italians in turn. They delighted in highlighting the self-satisfied irresponsibility of those who lived under the papal boot, their slovenly morals, their adamant laziness, their outrageous demands.

That being said, Gaspard was also poorly treated by the press in his home country. The French could not stand the idea that one of their own might aid the stupidest President in the history of that country. This was a time of transition—a small number of the French still believed in the benefits of intelligence. This wasn't to last, but Gaspard's promotion had come at the wrong time.

GOD AND THE BEARDED ONES

"Now I for one believe in God," said the President. "I'm a good Protestant."

The Protestants had formed a Christian sect, which became a religion. They didn't believe the Pope was God's representative on Earth or that he spoke with Him directly without the need of an intermediary.

More pragmatic, Catholics persisted in believing that God had too much going on, what with his holy wars and all, to attend to each and every person individually. They preferred appealing to one of the innumerable saints, less omnipotent but more inclined to take an interest in individual cases.

Saints proved to be important people in heaven who had won renown during their lifetimes through some spectacular act for the glory of God, generally speaking by dying in horrific agony.

"Hey there Gaspo my boy, do you believe in God?"

"No," replied Gaspard.

"Well then you don't believe in man either. When you don't believe in God, you can't believe in man, who is His creature. Unless you're a Nazi or a fucking commie. Now they believed in man without believing in God. But they lost. It was unavoidable. You can't believe in one without believing in the other."

"The bearded ones believe in God, but not so much in man," said Gaspard.

The bearded ones was a generic term used to refer to the Muslim god-fearers who bombed American skyscrapers with airliners and sowed terror among the non-believers. The

85

non-believers were those who didn't believe in their god. The bearded ones invoked Islam, a late-founded religion, but whose destiny perpetually seemed to be one civilization behind. Ever since their prophet threatened they'd find virgins in the great beyond, they had committed acts of war as life-saving masturbation. That made them both frightening and ridiculous.

Among themselves the bearded ones called each other *brothers*, in subliminal reference to Adolf the Kraut.

"I'll take care of the bearded ones," said the President. "I'm going to shoot a couple missiles up their asses."

The President adored vulgarities when he was in private. It was more laid-back.

"Believe you me, my little transatlantic frog. I'm gonna fucking light them up."

That's how Protestants were: they believed in predestination, and as the elect, by definition, would be but a tiny minority, they strongly suspected that their own individual chances remained mediocre. This made them morose, and as soon as they had well-made, sophisticated weapons at their disposal they were ready to declare war on anyone—communists, bearded ones, Copts, or animists.

The President scratched his nose.

This is the type of everyday gesture that one has to know how to place in a novel. It humanizes the character, and, as a result, the author himself.

The President scratched his nose.

"In God we trust," he said.

NATIONAL MOTTOS

IN GOD WE TRUST was the motto of the United States of America. A motto was a phrase whereby a given country would indicate to others what it found particularly important. Great Britain's was *God and my right.* Afghanistan's, *God is great.* Saudi Arabia's, *There is no other God than God.* Nauru's, *God's will first.* Denmark's, *God's help, Denmark's strength.* Chile's, *By reason or by force.* Pakistan's, *Faith and discipline.* Lebanon's, *My country is always right.* Austria's, *It is Austria's destiny to rule the world.*

And so on.

Besides mottos, countries had coats of arms, banners, ensigns, and flags. On solemn occasions they played their national anthem, a kind of song in their own honor. Subjects included the motherland, the courage of the ancients, glorious battles, the future that was almost here.

To my knowledge, the only exception to this rule was the Czech national anthem. My compatriots had rarely shone in the doleful firmament of humanity, but in this case, they had a stroke of genius. No glorious battles, no courage, no future in their national anthem. For their anthem they had chosen a lyrical verse from a lame nineteenth-century comedy—a verse sung by a blind man who, wielding his cane, would cross the stage while running into furniture and bleating: Where is my homeland? Where is my home?

ON CIVILIZATION

The motto of Luxembourg was *We wish to remain what we are.*

ON THE INCAN EMPIRE

THE ACT OF ADMITTING the collapse of a civilization was similar, according to Gaspard, to imagining our own death.

"Even though we have been informed from a very early age of the fact that our life will not continue eternally, our death, until a very late moment in life, is incomprehensible to us. We know, but we cannot grasp it. This also holds true for civilizations. We have been informed of the disappearance of the Incan Empire, the breakup of the Middle Kingdom, the death throes of the Roman Empire. But that our civilization might one day disappear?"

Over the years he had become, in the eyes of most of his former friends, *too nostalgic*—in other words, nostalgia being classified politically as right wing, passéist, backward-looking, declinist, reactionary, and to sum it up, *Islamophobic*—a popular expression of the day.

Being right wing signified, generally speaking, defending the idea that man is bound by more or less invariable values that existed before him, while being left wing meant believing in the benefits of re-education. For the last century and a half, politicians were enjoined to choose one view or another. Both sides undeniably failed, one just as crass as the other.

Before this, phobias were strictly the domain of psychological vocabulary, designating an unreasonable fear or instinctive aversion.

fear of	*aversion to*
the passage of time	*spiders*
the infinite	*public transportation*
night	*crowds*
premature ejaculation	*the human race*
etc.	*etc.*

From that moment hence, these were used to transform any disagreement into a deliberately hostile attitude. This allowed the holders of one opinion to highlight their rationality while making it known that their opponents had no place in a salubrious, well-balanced society.

In this way, advertising executives would label the few who resisted their nonsense as *advertiphobic*, and producers of idiotic television shows called dismayed viewers *mediaphobic*.

To get back to Islamophobia, semantic slippage transformed criticism of a particularly gynophobic religion into a particular xenophobia, and then into distinct racism.

Kind of like if an ice cream maker, who was proud of his recipe, had given birth to a race of strawberry ice cream worshippers in order then to label racist all those whom strawberry ice cream disgusted.

"You gonna eat your ice cream?"

"I don't like it."

"Racist!"

Have you had your breakfast, yet?

NOT SERIOUS

"THAT'S TOTALLY STUPID."

"I beg your pardon, sir?"

"Your comparisons. Faith in God and vanilla ice cream."

"Strawberry."

"It's the same thing."

"Not at all!"

"Really? Alright, if you say so."

"You see!"

"See what?"

"That they're not the same. It's never the same. There's a ton of different flavors."

"But it's not about ice cream."

"How's that?"

"You're putting faith and ice cream on the same playing field."

"Or on the same cone."

"Oh, I get it. You're being witty. You're trying to provoke me. You won't share."

Share, another very fashionable word at the time. People no longer debated, people no longer discussed, people no longer chatted, people no longer chewed the fat, people no longer joshed: people shared. It was, as they said, a sharing economy. This was a sign that humanity was appeased. Disseminating signs of appeasement was a specialty of European civilization ever since it had adopted the concept of the *self-fulfilling prophecy* as its own.

"I'm not married. But if you want to share your wife. . ."

"Seriously? Lame puns never move things forward. You're not being serious, and you're making fun of serious stuff."

"Who ever decreed that strawberry ice cream wasn't serious stuff?"

"See, there you go again."

"Okay, let's turn the argument around. Who decreed that faith was serious stuff?"

"It's part of human nature."

"So, no decree?"

"Faith doesn't need decrees."

"If I may, I wasn't talking about faith. I was talking about faith as serious stuff. There's a subtle difference there."

"I don't see the difference. On your deathbed you won't see one either."

"I know someone who asked for a toothpick on his deathbed. Those were his last words. Do you believe he wasn't serious?"

"Here we go. Now it's toothpicks."

"He could have just as easily asked for strawberry ice cream."

"Enough of your strawberry ice cream!"

"Oh, now you're the one who doesn't want to share."

"I don't share with troublemakers."

"That's too easy."

"Without faith, humanity would be fucked!"

"I agree. More or less. What remains to be determined is which faith, and in what."

"Certainly not in strawberry ice cream."

"Why not?"

"Because it's not serious!"

ON PORK

ANOTHER DAY, the President sent for Gaspard to have him taste a 1959 Lafite-Rothchild. Lafite-Rothchild was a prestigious and expensive French wine.

"Six thousand dollars a bottle," said the President. "I asked. And I've got others, way older, at a hundred twenty thou a pop. Whaddya think? I don't know about you, but I'd rather have a beer."

The President had before him two glasses. In order to compare he would alternate a swallow of Lafite-Rothchild with a swallow of Budweiser, a beer with a secondary fermentation whose lack of flavor made it relatively disfavored among European beer drinkers, but very popular in the United States.

Great swaths of Americans endowed with unpretentious palates thus brought joy to shameless slingers of swill.

"Nothing like a nice, frosty cold one with some baby back ribs."

Baby back ribs were an American specialty—meat from the ribs of a young pig taken from the upper thoracic cage between the spine and the spare ribs.

Then the conversation took a more cultural turn.

"You French, you know loads about chow, right?"

"More or less."

"That's 'cause you're Christians. Like us. Christians can eat anything, not like the Jews. What's it again they can't eat?"

"Pork. Among other things."

"But pork's so good. Especially with a frosty cold one. What's up with that?"

"It's rather complicated. It goes way back."

"And Muslims? Do they eat like us?"

"Except for pork."

"Ah, both Jews and Muslims don't eat pig?"

"No."

"But they're always getting the other's goat."

"It's complicated. It goes way back."

"Oh? They're not vegetarians at least, right?"

ON VEGETARIANS

THE PRESIDENT WAS was wary of vegetarians. While eating human flesh was generally viewed as reprehensible, vegetarians also prohibited eating the flesh of other vertebrates. Eating the flesh of other species was occasionally possible—mollusks, reptiles, fish, dragonflies. The majority of vegetarians also allowed themselves to eat eggs from other vertebrates because the embryo that the egg contained was not considered an animal—chicken eggs, penguin eggs, and so on. With humans, people spoke of an embryo during the first weeks of the organism's development, then of a fetus. Eating one or the other would have been considered perverse and immoral. Lastly, in some civilizations it was tacitly forbidden to eat the flesh of animals that were considered pets—dogs, cats, guinea pigs, and so on. In others it was acceptable.

	vegetarians	non-vegetarians	Chinese
vertebrates	−	+	+
mollusks	(+)	+	+
eggs	(+)	+	+
embryos or			
human fetuses	−	−	−
dogs	−	−	+
cats		−	+
guinea pigs	−	−	+

But a subset of vegetarians, called vegans, also avoided eating anything that came from the animal kingdom, regardless of its stage of development, including by-products:

	vegetarians	vegans
vertebrates	–	–
mollusks	(+)	–
eggs	(+)	–
embryos and human fetuses	–	–
guinea pigs	–	–
honey	+	–

What's more, in two of the three religions with a single god, it was in fact forbidden to eat the flesh of swine, commonly referred to as pork:

	Jews	Christians	Muslims
swine	–	+	–

However it was a Christian, Bernard of Clairvaux, who spoke of brother swine who lives within all men.

swine	*brother*	man

And it's this selfsame Bernard of Clairvaux who declared in anger, "Angels do not approve of the murder of Jews." A courageous man!

With Jewish god-fearers, it was also forbidden to eat the flesh of camels, rabbits, monkfish, eels, osprey, vultures, and bats. Jews were authorized to consume other animals, as long as they were slaughtered by authorized slaughterers. This requirement also held for Muslim god-fearers, for whom the head of the slaughtered animal needed to be turned toward Mecca, birthplace of the prophet, so that even the dying animals could pay him tribute.

For certain religions with multiple gods it was recommended to abstain from eating the flesh of wild beasts and birds of prey, for fear that humans would end up looking like what they eat.

---

		wild beasts
man	*swine*	
		birds of prey

According to the holy book of Jewish god-fearers, the first ten generations of man were vegetarians, obeying the will of God. Then God himself, for obscure reasons, changed the deal: henceforth man shall sustain himself on the flesh of animals—barring a few exceptions, for which please see above.

Later, during the nineteenth century, vegetarianism had become a doctrine whose goal was the renewal of humanity. As with electricity and the telegraph, vegetarianism was called upon to enlighten a brutish world, gradually transforming it into a harmonious world. Among the most famous vegetarians of the last two centuries was Adolf the Kraut. In spite of his abhorrence for Jews, Adolf couldn't help but share with them an aversion for the flesh of swine, vulture, or camel.

PIGMAN

ALONG WITH THE RISE of artificial intelligence, which had given computer systems intellectual capacities comparable to those of man and had led to the massive presence of thinking machines on the battlefield, the American army had financed a project whose objective was the implantation of a previously genetically modified human embryo inside a pig; the goal was to conceive a creature which, while entirely appearing to be a pig, would have the intellectual capacity necessary to be enlisted without qualms. The task was assigned to the National Institutes of Health.

After a number of failures, the experiment finally bore fruit. Two hundred and thirty-five days of gestation passed, and the pig, sixth trial in the series, dubbed Sam Six, opened its eyes and gazed innocently around the austere laboratory.

"Who am I? Where do I come from? Where am I going?" he said in American English.

It was a huge shock. Not only was the pig perfectly capable of fulfilling its duties in enemy territory, but, as a bonus, it could also distinctly feel metaphysical anxiety, which would help it understand the righteousness of its cause. The pig was dispatched to the intelligence branch, double time, where it received the appropriate training and was soon deployed to China.

The National Institutes of Health then tackled cockroach-man—cockroaches being one of the rare creatures that can survive a nuclear war.

THE JOKE ABOUT THE TWO CHINESE, PART TWO

THE WAITER from the joke about the two Chinese returned several minutes later. The gentleman said, "How much do I owe you?" The waiter answered, "Two euros and sixty cents."

The gentleman, "Including tip?"

The waiter, offended, "Of course, sir."

I'll tell you the next part some other time.

ON SCURRILITY IN
A GLOBALIZED WORLD

IN A GLOBALIZED WORLD, jokes involving race, ethnicity, nationality, socio-economic condition, physical appearance, or sexual orientation were considered scurrilous and hurtful. In order to promote a harmonious society, interdictions multiplied. In order to avoid any kind of stigmatization, it was necessary to avoid offending the sensibilities of others. In order not to offend the sensibilities of others, **political correctness** was invented. From that point on it was a matter of erasing from language anything that might have symbolically harmed a minority group— jokes, scurrilous statements, hurtful comments. Given that, with the exception of heterosexuals, all human beings had become minorities in one way or another, this complicated things considerably. Those who continued making scurrilous statements were forced to specify that their statements were only scurrilous in appearance and that in reality they didn't believe what they were saying. What became the obligatory follow-up was, "I'm only joking."

Black people can run fast.
I'm only joking.

Germans have no sense of humor.
I'm only joking.

Russians drink like fishes.
I'm only joking.

Dwarfs have huge schlongs.
I'm only joking.

Chinese people have slanty eyes from eating rice.
I'm only joking.

For those who wished to send scurrilous jokes or statements to their friends via electronic message systems, new combinations of letters and diacritical marks were established so that the addressee would be in no doubt as to the good-natured intentions of the sender.

:P   Heeheehee.
:)   Hahaha.
:D   Hahahaha.
;)   I'm only joking.

Black people can run fast. :P
Chinese people have slanty eyes from eating rice. :)
Dwarfs have huge schlongs. :D
Hey, does your wife's carpet match the drapes? ;)

Humor was safe and sound.

ON OBJECTS

"So, they're believers?"

"They have to pray five times a day."

"That's understandable. Now five times a day might be too much, but God likes that. What else?"

"They also have to complete a pilgrimage to Mecca. At least once in their lives."

"That's in Africa, right?"

"Sort of."

"What else?"

"They have to respect their wives. Provide for their needs."

"That's normal."

"They have to avoid getting too close to the wives of others. And with married women in general."

"How close is too close?"

"I don't know. I'm working from memory here."

"Anything else?"

"When they sneeze, they have to say, 'Praise be to Allah.'"

"That's an odd way to pay homage to God. Keep going."

"They mustn't touch an object that has been previously touched by an unknown woman."

"What do you mean? What object?"

"Any object."

"And what do they do when they go shopping and there's some female at the cash register?"

"I don't think they're regulars at those kinds of places."

"This is getting better and better. What else?"

"Also, they must not shake the hands of unfamiliar women that they've met by chance or female colleagues in the countries where they work."

"They don't shake women's hands?"

"No."

"Then how do they fuck?"

The question was strange. Perhaps it said a great deal about the President's views on mating.

"You need other bits for that."

Gaspard was trying to be witty.

"Obviously. But if I want to fuck some unknown woman, I gotta shake her hand first. To introduce myself."

"We have to assume they do it differently there."

"That's poor manners. And stupid. And it definitely proves I'm right not to trust them."

RESEARCH

PIERRE-MAURICE VICTOR ÉMIEL BOISVERT launched the quest for his long-lost father in the mid-nineteen seventies, twenty or so years after his mother's death. There was one certainty—he was illegitimate. There was one probability—his father was a German soldier. There was one piece of information from his mother—his father was Adolf the Kraut, the most skilled murderer of all time.

Assuming that parents lie to their children at least as frequently as children to their parents, Pierre-Maurice remained unconvinced. The fact that over the years his mother had become an alcoholic, a hypochondriac, and a pathological liar also came into consideration. But even an alcoholic hypochondriacal mythomaniac can occasionally let slip some unexpected truth.

Once the decision was made, Pierre-Maurice enlisted the services of a historian, a certain Duval-Depuis, a self-proclaimed specialist in Franco-German relations during World War I and author of the book *Europe was Born in Women's Wombs*. Then he contacted a Parisian lawyer, Maître Anglade. Then he sought expertise in identification through comparative physiognomy at the Institute of Anthropology and Genetics at the University of Heidelberg. Then he commissioned a comparative psychographic study from the Department of Psychobiology at the University of Saarbrücken. That was all he could do at the time. Genealogical research by means of deoxyribonucleic acid sample, a molecule that carries genetic information, was not yet mature.

He conscientiously completed the form prepared by Duval-Depuis:

- *How tall are you?*
- *What is your blood type?*
- *What illness(es) do you have, and how long have you had it/them?*
- *Do you have two normally developed testicles?*
- *Do you like dogs?*
- *Do you like cats?*
- *Do you like animals in general?*
- *Do you like Jews?*
- *If not, do you at least have one Jewish friend?*
- *Are you a racist?*
- *If yes, why?*
- *If no, why not?*
- *Did you ever feel, during your youth, the desire to devote yourself to painting?*
- *Are you a vegetarian?*
- *If yes, why?*

He had returned to Pecquencourt, in the north of France, to rummage through attics and question his mother's few remaining former neighbors. His vocabulary ended up being enriched by several entirely new insults pronounced in the Picard dialect by the neighborhood shrews. Once that German Bastard Boy, always that German Bastard Boy. The Franco-German honeymoon, decreed in 1957 through the creation of a fraternal and economic community, had gone unnoticed in the region.

"I had before me a man who constantly hesitated between the desire to know everything and the desire to let it all drop," Maître Anglade would later say.

After eighteen months of investigations, Pierre-Maurice did decide to let it all drop. His sudden notoriety in the media was tormenting him. He had expected a discreet inquiry. That was without taking into account those he had called upon for the investigation. Duval-Depuis inundated historical journals with articles to bolster his reputation. Maître Anglade strutted in front of the television cameras three times a week.

Yet despite all that, his story didn't catch on in France. In

Germany, however, it had elicited a certain level of interest. The Germans liked the idea that Adolf might have had descendants, even if it was with a questionable race.

ON LANGUAGE

"THEY'RE MY NUMBER ONE PRIORITY," said the President.

The subject was the bearded ones.

Then, mysteriously, "You have to know how to anticipate things in advance."

The more unlettered they are, the more politicians peddle pleonasms.

He could have added, "We are going to take firm, bold positions which should eventually allow us to foresee on the horizon of the decision-making process a quick exit to the crisis." But he stopped speaking, mysteriously.

The Savior came to the world as Word incarnate, but as one of his friends later wrote, the world did not hear him. After the inaudible Logos had come the era of the thundering Epilogos—mistreated, lapidated, eviscerated, assassinated, overwhelmed—this was the Word at the turn of the century.

"More and more frequently I feel like I've been dropped into a town full of crazy people where language doesn't have the same meaning it has elsewhere."

In short, language was evolving. Faithful to its charge of giving expression to current thoughts, it had become doddering. Orators whose imbecility would melt the glaciers of the Antarctic circulated through the streets with complete impunity. They knew they had won: by dint of being taken as imbeciles, people had become imbeciles.

ON THE NEXT WORLD WAR

THE CHINESE, just like the Americans, were wild about baby back ribs. That should have facilitated intercultural dialogue and the establishment of direct and friendly relations. But American military experts were of the opinion that the next—unavoidable—world war would pit the United States against China, the former refusing to cede its status as a superpower to the latter. All of this in the context of what political pundits called a *major rift*: differences in form of government—democracy versus totalitarianism—just like in the past. The American experts had calculated that the war would produce 1,085,000,000 deaths and would be won by the United States.

It had started with skirmishes in the Yellow Sea.

THE SECRET PENTAGON REPORT

THIS WAS THE REPORT that the American President had Gaspard read.

"Well?" asked the President several days later. "Isn't it awesome? My boys predicted all that. It's rock solid."

Gaspard had engaged in a well-reasoned critique. But he had gone about it the wrong way.

"According to the introduction, this report is a summary of

debates from experts in the field. Which is exactly the problem. The participants in this type of collective work are invariably chosen according to one criterion—their willingness to submit to the concepts that are submitted to them. These people make a point of preemptively suppressing any objections fundamental to a contradictory point of view."

And so on.

SPECIALIST ENGLAND

"Who's ready to die for democracy? No one anymore, except for Lynndie England, of course."

At twenty-one years of age, Lynndie England was a Specialist in the American army that the President had sent to Iraq, a totalitarian country in the Middle East. The goal was to promote democracy so that the bearded ones would become voters. Posted to the 372nd Military Police Company, she was sentenced to three years in prison for humiliating treatment inflicted on detainees. She liked to walk them naked on a dog leash, force them to masturbate or masturbate them herself, or gather them in groups of six or seven in a pile of frightened, naked flesh. She was discharged from the army despite rallying cries from American citizens who had stressed how destabilizing defending democracy in a faraway country could be for an inexperienced young woman. Before being recruited by the army, they said, Lynndie England had regularly attended church.

It is entirely to the United States' honor, the President later declared, to see those who dishonor the American army brought to justice. He was right. The others didn't make such a fuss. But it was definitely too late to convince them of the benefits of Western democracy. Being tortured—the bearded ones were willing to accept that. What was unacceptable was being tortured by a woman.

SAME GOES FOR ME

I, TOO, COULD have become an advisor to a president, albeit a less important one than Gaspard's and less stupid. He was a former dissident who had become President of the Republic. In the formerly communist countries of Eastern Europe during the 1990s, it was the in-thing. Dissidents were people who had demonstrated their opposition to the dominant ideology while waiting for it to collapse. My president was one of the most well-known dissidents of his time. He'd asked me to be an advisor, or perhaps the minister of something, or maybe ambassador somewhere. But I had my translation of *Pantagruel* to finish up.

Both communism and capitalism envisioned an ever-brighter future. The only difference was in the form. Capitalism promised happiness to the rich while letting the poor hope one day to join their ranks. Communism promised happiness to all provided they stayed poor for a good while.

CLIMATE CHANGE, PART TWO

THE REPORTS NEVER STOPPED. The President would pull out two or three a week.

"I've got another one," he said. "Special Report: Climate Change."

Climate change was a major topic at the beginning of the last millennium. It would bring about massive emigration toward more temperate zones in the Northern Hemisphere. Added to the exoduses of those fleeing holy wars and several hundred million Chinese fleeing China, it was going to end up being a real shit show.

"Warming planet, you know, that kind of stuff. Oceans over-flowing, abandoned ski resorts. Here."

And then handing Gaspard a file embossed with the seal of the United States, a kind of raptor holding an olive branch in one claw and a bundle of arrows in the other, one side symbolizing peace, the other war—or perhaps the successful extermination of the American Indian.

In the old days Indians were a race composed of various tribes—the Arapaho, Sioux, Crow, Cheyenne, Shoshone, Kiowa, Apache, and several others. The whole coterie had been merrily waging war against one another for the last five thousand years. Then the Protestants landed and massacred them all in order to open the door for their *way of life*. Once the heathens had been eradicated from the face of the Earth, happiness in the fear of God would be henceforth available to all.

113

"Between you and me, Gaspard my little Froggie, I believe in it about this much."

The four centimeters separating his thumb and index finger indicated the meager faith the President held in the dangers of climate change.

"It's fucking global warming that made civilization possible, right? Sedenratization and all that."

"Sedentarization."

"If you will. In any case, beforehand, according to what people say, we were all a bunch of fucking nomadic monkeys."

Gaspard didn't respond.

"I for one believe in wars," said the President. "Wars are concrete. You win 'em or you lose 'em. Now us, we win 'em. Global warming my ass. But hush hush, eh? Your clown of a President'll make a big stink."

The then French President liked to speak ill of his American counterpart. This had tarnished the cordial relations the two countries traditionally maintained.

ON THE FRENCH

FOR MANY YEARS the French had been convinced that, in comparison to other nations, they were the most intelligent. They were wrong, but only halfway. They were the least stupid. For to be able to judge the IQ of a nation, the proper scale to apply is not that of reason, but rather stupidity. Being the most intelligent country in the world by no means excludes stupidity.

Later they had changed their minds, then believing themselves to be less intelligent than others. They were wrong, but only halfway. They'd become just as stupid.

In the past, the path toward lesser stupidity was achieved through cultural means. Culture was a body of knowledge that allowed the development of critical sensibility. It seemed important at the time.

In France it was used as symbolic currency in social relationships. A speaker's worth was based on his ability to appear cultured. There was a time when this was shared, more or less, by the rest of the Western world, and even beyond. But little by little France found itself increasingly alone, the last vanity of a lost world, the last glory of the ancients' fantasies, the final scrap of an illusion mired in the thick and self-satisfied inculture of the rest of the world.

That is when the French, recognizing their isolation, had started to imitate others with just as much stupidity, although, in the short term, without the desired effectiveness. You have to allow one or two generations for stupidity to settle in once and for all. But a new method soon came into existence that taught ambitious people to express themselves like idiots in order to become popular and indispensable. Various education ministers had formulated teaching reforms. One of them summarized these in a phrase that became famous for its forthrightness: *"Handing cultural knowledge down to our children is tantamount to making them unfit for social life."*

ON TRUE STUPIDITY

IN SHORT, the French had, over the course of two or three centuries, suffered from an excess of intelligence. Excess intelligence impedes the recognition of stupidity and thus the ability to resist it. So, after a certain point intelligence becomes stupid enough to consider stupidity just as clever as intelligence. It then in turn becomes stupid itself, albeit something very narrowly focused, incapable of analyzing things. Intelligence that has turned to stupidity is only obtuse. True stupidity, however, is both obtuse and wily, and endowed with considerable analytical capacity. Take the Czechs—they were clearly less intelligent than the French, and, consequently, more able to resist the stupidity of others.

Wily stupidity is insufferable. But stupidity without wiliness is frightening.

JEWISH MERCHANTS

"So, you're claiming that Jesus was Jewish?"

"I am not claiming it, Mr. President. Apparently, I am teaching you it, sir."

"But not Jewish like the others?"

"Oh, yes. Like the others."

"No, I mean, when I say not like the others, not Jewish Jewish."

"Yes, Jewish Jewish."

"But he drove them out! He drove the Jews out of their temple there! It's in the New Testament!"

The New Testament was the holy book of Christian god-fearers. The main character of which was the Savior who during His time championed the idea that all men had some kind of soul. He was betrayed and killed so that humanity might become happy and healthy. No one has ever been able to give a single reason for His devotion to the human race.

"Not the Jews. The Jewish merchants."

"You see! That's what I was telling you! A Jewish merchant's still a Jew. And doubly so!"

GASPARD THE URANIST

THE AUTOCHTHONOUS ADVISORE' animosity got the better of Gaspard's career just a short eight months after he took up his new position. From the first few weeks they accused him of not playing the game. *Playing the game* was a popular phrase at the time, infantilizing to the extent that it conjoined two childish words in one expression that didn't mean much of anything. Expressed in the negative, it designated an individual who was also negative, who didn't participate in the established—but never required—rituals. Yet these rituals proved the loyalty of an individual to an established body, to a network of direct friendships. The lack of allegiance to this network of clear-cut friendships constituted, symbolically speaking, the ultimate crime.

It didn't gel. Box of Matches was watching over him. She had managed to persuade her uncle that Gaspard's attitude was in fact proof of his exceptional commitment. The king's jester had no use for social rituals.

But the advisors would not admit defeat and ended up finding what they believed was a home run. Through subterfuges of various levels of sophistication, they started a whisper campaign to the press that if being French wasn't bad enough, Gaspard was a homosexual to boot, or more precisely: light in the loafers, a *merry* chap, a *gladsome* bloke, a *jolly* old soul, a *lavender* lover, a *wimbly-wambly* guy, a mollycoddler, a uranist, a fag. It was false, but henceforth true.

Consequently, the President ran the risk of having his fellow

Americans consider him at best depraved, and, at worst, a flaming poofter. Ties were immediately severed.

"I should have suspected it," said the President. "But when I think about it now, he did give me some funny looks once in a while."

SYMPTOMS ALLEVIATED

BACK IN PARIS, Gaspard had experienced his first memory lapses. At the same time he showed himself to be what psychologists call an *unstable* subject—someone who has difficulty maintaining a lasting mental state, someone who changes his behavior like the weather.

So, along with his bouts of guarded optimism, Gaspard would become aggressive. He would attend public meetings in his neighborhood, philosophical discussions in cafés, debates organized by associations founded on the assumption that man is naturally good—insuperable according to Gaspard, which experience refutes not only on a daily basis but also during those moments qualified as historically significant. He was always willing to speak and would frequently become aggressive, insulting people left and right. Certain claims, even though generally innocuous overall, would make his blood boil. They were the issues of the day: democracy and its limits, authoritarian and totalitarian regimes, religion, education, the media, women's place in society. Have you had your breakfast, yet?

One day he roughed up a lecturer who had been explaining that female circumcision was first and foremost a cultural act, and that it should be treated as such—with the respect that people who respect culture in general should respect in this specific instance.

"FGM, that is, female genital mutilation, let's be careful, I'm not making any excuses. That's not what I'm saying. But it's true, it's clearly first and foremost a cultural act and, clearly, we don't want to fall into ethnocentrism or paternalism. First and foremost we should treat it as . . ."

He didn't have the time to complete his thought. Gaspard, who, opportunely, was seated in the first row, had flung himself at the man, grabbed him by the ears, and started shaking him like a baby.

"Oh yeah? And stoning chicks, that's a cultural act, too?"

"Are you, crazy? You've got it all mixed up! Stop it, dammit!"

The incident energized the room. People were enjoying themselves. They vociferously manifested their disapprobation.

Another time Gaspard hurled a folding chair at the head of a young sociologist who claimed that the media were independent in democratic countries. The young woman had just published her thesis, *The Role of Modern Media in the Conception of Democratic Thought*. She was extremely shocked by Gaspard's violently antidemocratic act.

Nevertheless, the incident energized the room. People vociferously manifested their disapprobation.

Another time it was a professor who had come to inform the audience that Western democracy represented the final stage of advanced society. Another time it was a trade union official who declared that in any advanced society the advent of communism was inevitable. Another time it was a potbellied fifty-year-old who was explaining to the crowd the difference between a *burqa* and a *niqab*. Another time it was an economist who claimed that in the long run capitalism was beneficial to all. Another time it was a hepatologist lecturing on healthy living and the ill-effects of overindulgence. Another time it was a former women's javelin champion who contended that sport is a vector for values. And so on and so forth. And each time the room was energized.

Strangely enough, not only was there nothing premeditated in Gaspard's actions, but once the incident was over, he didn't remember a thing. Barely a shadow of a memory of some sort of confusion. A memory lapse after a night of drunken revelry. Distraught, he had consulted a psychiatrist.

"Here ya go, a little Prozac for six weeks. Very effective in the treatment of minor depressive symptoms. Don't you worry about it."

Prozac was a minimally toxic antidepressant. Doctors prescribed it for melancholia, depression, anxiety, disillusionment, and consternation. Once the symptoms were neutralized, the patient would rediscover his purpose in life. He would return to being calm and happy.

BY THE HORNS

THE QUEST FOR HAPPINESS was another of modern Western society's ideas. In the past, it had generally been accepted that there was no happiness on this Earth. Even in the great beyond, beatitude—less frightening and more eternal—had been prudently substituted for it.

But this was before the advent of progress. Progress was the idea that society gradually transformed toward the better, and eventually toward the best. It was progress that paved the way for humanity's evolution and individual happiness. People had grabbed it by the horns. The reason it hadn't existed hitherto was because it had been conceptualized as inert, immobile. Let's make it ever-evolving, continuous, perpetual. Let's have it move, like the world, like progress itself, and dagnabbit, it'll have to start existing.

Dagnabbit was a favorite expression of those who were prone to optimism.

And it worked. All kinds of happiness started to flourish. *Utilitarianism*, maximal happiness for a maximal number of people. *Marxism*, happiness for workers. *The Way of Life*, happiness in proportion to one's level of consumption.

And so on.

Gee, ain't that swell.

VARIED SYMPTOMS

THE PROZAC HAD NO EFFECT on Gaspard. After six weeks of treatment not only did he still not understand what was happening to him at those meetings, but also he fell into an even deeper depression. Depression was the disease of the century, whence the Prozac. But, rather curiously, depressive states manifested themselves in distinct ways in different parts of the world—shame and guilt in the West, digestive issues in Africa, feelings of persecution in the Middle East, apathy and refusal to eat in China. Symptoms varied. But Gaspard seemed to combine them all at once.

ON DESPAIR

*"When hopelessness
takes a dip,
when hope sometimes
lets one rip. . ."*

THE POEM, cited in one of Gaspard's notebooks, was the work of a Czech author, Jan Zabrana, which I had previously translated for an anthology, *Cutting the Silence*, published in 1992 by Temps Perdu. I'd sent him a copy.

"We don't vet anything anymore. We're caught in a gigantic landslide, and no one gives a damn."

A few weeks after his return to Paris, we met up at a sidewalk café on rue Saint-Maur in the eleventh arrondissement. The world was falling apart, but it was still possible to meet up at a sidewalk café.

That day, at five o'clock in the afternoon, we enumerated one hundred and eighteen armed conflicts in the world and just as many moronic shows on every television channel that God hath created.

SPIRITUALITY

"THE PROBLEM, if I may, is that you're too spiritual. Spirituality and mental health have fuzzy contours, you see, quite fuzzy, and any attempt at a definition is tricky. Let's just say spirituality looks for meaning in life by opposing itself, you know, to materialism. But here's the thing, it finds its converse in the existential nihilism of life's meaninglessness, which itself calls mental health into question. You move, you see, from a logic of living, of thriving, to a logic of surviving. And in order to avoid deception, you know, your revolt takes on the form of a destructive rage. I have to admit I was wrong. It wasn't just a simple depression."

"Adolf Hitler was my grandfather. Maybe."

"Oh?" responded the psychiatrist. "Do you have a talent for painting?"

ON SUICIDES

AT THAT TIME several categories of suicide had been identified:

A. Philosophical Suicide. Whereas life is absurd, the ultimate incoherency would be to carry on.

B. Existential Suicide. From a certain age—having accomplished all that one set out to accomplish, why be bored any longer?

C. Narcissistic Suicide. To make others know that one existed.

D. Melancholic Suicide. When every second of every day becomes unbearable.

These categories were not mutually exclusive. With Gaspard, I'd bet on an A/D variation.

People also talked about altruistic suicide. While he was at it, the suicide would practice suicide on those near and dear to him—his wife, his children, his dog—to remove from life those he loved, a bit like some Gnostics, who, in days of yore, peregrinated throughout Europe killing people out of empathy in order to deliver them from the misery of terrestrial life. I can easily imagine that Gaspard, had he been born nineteen hundred years earlier, might have been one of them.

But he had neither wife nor child, and his dog had died long ago.

The various religions, for once in agreement on something, considered suicide to be an offense against God. It was up to Him, and Him alone, to effectuate our death.

	philo-sophical suicide	exis-tential suicide	narcis-sistic suicide	melan-cholic suicide	altruistic suicide
Jewish religion	no	no	no	no	no
Christian religion	no	no	no	no	no
Muslim religion	no	no	no	no	no
Brahminic religions, etc.	no	no	no	no	no
Gaspard	yes	no	no	yes	yes?

The martyr, classified in the subcategory of narcissistic suicide by psychoanalysts, was not considered as such by religions with only one god, and, during my time, especially not by the Muslim religion. Those who committed suicide by killing a large number of miscreants had only seemed to die. They would remain forever living in the great beyond, enjoying limitless delights for all eternity.

ON MARTYRDOM

ORIGINALLY, martyr simply meant *witness* and *martyrdom* testimony. Once again, a poor translation would bring suffering and grief to the world. The first martyr catalogued by the Christian god-fearers was the deacon Stephen, a scholar and haranguer. But, by continually haranguing crowds he had become annoying. The crowd, disgruntled, drove him to the city gates, pummeled him with insults, called him dull and a snooze, and lapidated him.

ON INSULTS

AMONG THE INSULTS that I needed to learn in order to prove at a moment's notice my successful integration into the French nation, there's one I was particularly fond of: *asshole.* Simply calling someone an ass wouldn't have had the same impact. An ass is an ass, and forever shall be. The genius move is the hole. The lack. The absence. Nothingness.

The insult is philosophical.

"One last time, sir, how can our consciousness be part of the world? How can it face various objective transcendences? I ask you how?"

"Yo, I got your transcendence right here, asshole!"

BLONDI, HELGA, AND THE OTHERS

As for Adolf, he committed suicide with his dog and his mistress after having lost the war. His successor as leader of Germany, a man by the name of Joseph Goebbels, committed suicide the following day with his wife and their children. The dog was named Blondi, the mistress, Eva. Joseph's wife was named Magda. The children were named Helga, Hilde, Helmut, Holde, Hedda, and Heide. Magda and Joseph liked names that started with H. But the children would get confused. When their parents called for Heide, Hilda would come running. When they summoned Hedda, Helga would appear. Only Helmut never got mixed up.

Following their wishes, the bodies of Adolf, Joseph, and the two women were burned. Blondi was buried in a shell crater. The five pups she'd birthed a few weeks before were gathered up by Adolf's dog-handler, Sergeant-Major Fritz. The Russians captured the Sergeant and killed the pups by crushing their skulls against the side of a tank.

The bodies of Joseph and Magda's children were found intact. The Russians burned them and scattered the ashes in the Elbe, a Czech river.

ON ABILITY

HAVING PERFORMED an autopsy on Adolf's calcined corpse, the Russians claimed that during his lifetime he had had but a single testicle.

Normally testicles came in pairs. They were called nuts, stones, balls, nads, dangly bits, cojones, misters, lemons, family jewels; in recipes they became Rocky Mountain oysters or calf fries and were frequently served with a Madeira wine sauce. *Having balls* was an expression that referred to a courageous man, someone determined, able to get things done. *Grow a pair*, on the other hand, indicated a man who lacked courage, someone without determination. But, reviewing Adolf's case, psychologists concluded that for him to have reached his singular destiny it was a good thing he didn't have a pair. It was precisely the absence of a second nad, they said, that was at the origin of Adolf's exceptional speaking ability.

All in all, psychology was a rather useless, albeit pleasant science, which had its moment of glory during the twentieth century.

ON VIAGRA

THE COMPLEMENT to Prozac in the Western man's search for happiness was sildenafil, a medication classified as a phosphodiesterase inhibitor and developed and commercialized under the brand name Viagra. It came into the world at the end of the next-to-last century. Originally, the pharmaceutical research was focused on a treatment for angina pectoris, but in clinical trials the observed effect was basically nil. But a secondary effect, quite unplanned, was that the medicine induced an erection. In a nutshell, the patient would be suffering from pains in the chest, up and down the arm, in the back, the neck, the jaw, but would be as hard as a wandering knight. So the lab decided to drop the angina pectoris and sell their happy little accident to the needy.

AMAZING PILLS
IN TROPICAL FRUIT FLAVORS!
JUST TEN MINUTES
TO GET YOUR MANLINESS BACK!

DIFFERENT FLAVORED GELCAPS
THAT DISOLVE EVEN MORE QUICKLY
ALLOWING YOU TO ATTAIN
A HARD ERECTION
IN JUST A COUPLE MINUTES!

"Is there such a thing as a soft erection?"

"Who knows. These days, you know you got to be ready for anything."

If I'd been a marketing consultant for the maker of Viagra, I would've drawn from my studies in philosophy:

KANT OR CUNT? VIAGRA FOR THE WIN!

Besides Viagra, couples demanding steamy nights and uninhibited sensual delights would use various objects designed to augment carnal pleasure. They were called *sex toys*.

THE TOYS THAT DRIVE US CRAZY:

Inflate to the desired size
Delightfully large
A welcoming chest for wild nights
Vibrating egg for spicy evenings
Soft testicles
It ejaculates!
It moves back and forth!
The ticklish hairs will make you shudder with pleasure
Sliding foreskin!

UNDESIREABLE SIDE EFFECTS

Prozac	*Viagra*
diarrhea	diarrhea
dizziness	dizziness
nausea	fainting
abnormal vision	abnormal vision
migraines	migraines
micturition issues	nasal congestion
cardiac issues	myocardial infarction (*rare*)
auditory hallucinations	hearing issues or loss
visual hallucinations	indigestion
convulsions	circulatory issues
myoclonus	myoclonus
fever	fever
insomnia	erythema
hemorrhaging	cyanosis
decreased libido	priapism

ON MONGOLIA

AT THE TIME, several Western media outlets wondered whether the American President was simply stupid or whether he was crazy. According to several observers, his mental state appeared to present every symptom of a clinical illness, specifically the condition known as Nero syndrome. Nero was the sovereign of an ancient power, the Roman Empire, who supposedly sent his henchmen to set fire to various public buildings in Rome in order to destroy the city so that he could then rebuild it as the city of Neropolis, even more beautiful and majestic than before. Nero syndrome thus designated a megalomaniacal individual possessing considerable political power and guided in his actions by destructive impulses. His misdeed done, Nero reportedly accused the Christians, whom he called dirty Jews. It is said that he cast several hundred in the lion pits to appease the population.

Stupid or crazy, soon after Gaspard's return to France the American President had decided to conduct the test firing of a surface-to-surface missile from a submarine that was meandering around the Pacific, aiming the bomb at Mongolia. As Mongolia was the least densely populated country in the world, this was considerate. But the Chinese and the Russians took it badly.

ON HISTORY

"Where is the wood?
Where is the resin?
The city burns at noon!"

THE NATIONAL ANTHEM OF MALTA

SEVERAL YEARS LATER, while conflicts related to water supply questions were multiplying, while streams of Caribbean refugees were infiltrating the southern United States and tensions were mounting along the border with Mexico, while Indian and Chinese warships were on constant alert in the Persian Gulf, while a civil war was erupting in China and a clan war in Saudi Arabia, while Japan and Russia were arguing over energy resources on the Island of Sakhalin, while the European Union was no longer anything but the painful memory of a few idealists, while skirmishes between France and Germany over commercial access to the Rhine were becoming more and more violent, while the Serbs had once again invaded Croatia and the Argentineans the British Overseas Protectorate, while the exclave of Kaliningrad had declared its independence and Russian tanks were once again crossing Poland and the Baltic States, while the death count in sub-Saharan Africa was stopped due to a lack of reliable data, while micro black holes were multiplying like rabbits and gobbling up everything within reach, and while the first mass extinction in the history of the Earth directly realized by a living species was soon to come to pass, the bearded ones, according to secret Pentagon reports, were getting ready to invade Malta. The President of the Republic had called a state of emergency and stationed armed guards in the fortified towers, which had been built previously to prevent Barbary pirates from pillaging the island's riches and raping any female they found.

Every day at noon, the national anthem of Malta rang out from the ramparts:

Lil din l-Art helwa, l-Omm li tatna isimha!
Hares Mulej, kif dejjem Int harist!
Ftakar li lilha bl-ohla dawl libbist!

Aghti kbir Alla, id-deh'n lil min jahkimha!
Rodd il-hniena lis-sid, sahha'l-haddiem!
Seddaq il-ghaqda fil-Maltin u s-sliem!

ON THE PLANETS

AT THE SAME TIME, lacking other ideas, planetologists were looking for a planet to which a portion of the population could migrate before their complete destruction. They located planets where water could be found in a liquid state and classified them according to the areas fit for habitation: life was possible there, another world could be imagined, without bearded ones or fags, without Jews or the homeless, without writers or poor workers, without wars or violence. For the colonizers would be chosen following very strict genealogical guidelines, their genetic makeup modified as necessary, their moral sensibility strengthened.

PHOTOGRAPH

TAKE A GOOD HARD LOOK at this photograph. Here you will find a glimpse of the state of Western civilization in the 2020s.

DIALOGUE

I REMEMBER a bit of dialogue from a film:
"This all merits reflection."
"Yes, boss. I've already started."

MORE DIALOGUE

I REMEMBER another bit of dialogue from a film:
  "What are you doing here?"
  "Nothing."

RESEARCH, PART TWO

AFTER SEVERAL YEARS' hesitation, Gaspard had resumed the genealogical search for his father. No need to look for indirect proof or respond to idiotic questionnaires. With paternity tests based on deoxyribonucleic acid, things had become much simpler. All you had to do was make an appointment with a professional, in this case Dr. Morelli, a specialist in forensic medicine. A few years beforehand, he had even supposedly identified the skull of Henri IV, a French king during the wars of religion. Dr. Morelli took a sample of Gaspard's saliva, extracted the white blood cells, analyzed the deoxyribonucleic acid, and the game was on.

It remained to procure some of Adolf the Kraut's DNA. Impossible. The Russians, after recovering the incinerated body and burying what was left, had eventually changed their minds and decided to exhume and burn it a second time, or what was left of it. This earned them the reputation of being particularly spiteful people.

That being the case, it was necessary to convince several still-living specimens of Adolf's genealogy to provide their DNA. The family tree was especially lush. Since a certain Johannes, who died in 1703, eight generations, one hundred forty descendants, and twenty-one liters of sperm had been necessary finally to bring about the birth of little Adolf.

In Austria, Dr. Morelli eventually found two more or less distant relatives who had agreed to provide DNA samples.

Tests were conducted. The verdict was incontrovertible.

Impatient readers will find it in the chapter entitled *The Verdict*.

Those who love suspense will wait patiently.

GASPARD LOSES HIS MEMORY

THEN THE IMPLAUSIBLE HAPPENED—the memory lapses had metamorphosed into complete amnesia. Quite an odd story. At the time Gaspard was living with Rose while still retaining his tub apartment, seeking refuge there fairly regularly to translate.

He had met Rose several years before. Thirteen years his junior, she owed her rosy name to the political activism of her parents, who were born in the middle of the last century and became what are known as sixty-eighters, in reference to the events that took place in France and elsewhere in 1968. Bourgeois teens with time on their hands had had their cultural revolution. Starting as members of the Anarchist Federation, her parents then veered toward communism. The choice of their daughter's name was an homage to Rosa Luxemburg, a militant socialist who lived at the turn of the twentieth century and who was assassinated by a bullet in the head on 15 January 1919, which was, moreover, the five hundred fiftieth anniversary of the resumption of the Hundred Years' War.

Rose, after a childhood and adolescence spent among aging young revolutionaries who would traipse around the apartment naked and from time to time break into "We Shall Overcome," had a crush on a journalist of sorts, who worked as a freelancer. They'd had a son whom they named Ernest in homage to Ernesto Guevara, a South American guerilla from the 1950s, revolutionary court prosecutor, and creator of re-education camps for those who cared for revolution not a whit. Sometime later the freelancer had become the managing editor of a weekly magazine

147

that conformed to the tastes of the day, and, swapping his dissidence for the advantages of Western society, he distanced himself from both the errors of his youth and his partner.

Rose, finding herself alone with her son and never having attended college—an invention of the ruling class the better to dominate the ruled—scraped by doing odd jobs, until the day when, coming home with Ernest from a demonstration in support of illegal immigrants (she had the kindheartedness to take at face value the stories of persecution and misery that debonair blacks, affable Asians, and viriloid Afghans told her), she found herself in the wrong place at the wrong time. A bomb exploded in the middle of Paris, which blew off her leg and killed Ernest instantly. This happened in July 1995. A group of Muslim god-fearers claimed responsibility for the attack, which was designed to show their willingness to fight the heathens.

Rose received an articulated prosthesis and a disability pension.

She had run into Gaspard at several meetings in the neighborhood and had appreciated his violent reactions to the speakers.

ON YOUTH

THE CHILDREN BORN as a result of the copulations of the generation of sixty-eight were later bound to rebuke their parents for having had an easier life than they did, struggling to find a job in a world gone mad. No work, no dough. No home theater, no expensive drugs, no Viagra, not even a couch.

They rebuked their parents for having known a time when being naive was considered a positive attribute. For believing, even if only briefly, that humanity was good. For having done exciting stuff—raising hell, shooting up all day, fucking and sucking for hours on end.

In short, they rebuked their parents for having been freer than they were.

In my home country young people also criticized their parents. Yet young people there were infinitely freer than their parents, who had been damaged by forty years of stupid and viscous totalitarian rule. Nevertheless, all things considered, they believed their parents' lives were easier than theirs because the very essence of a totalitarian regime is to take charge of its subjects' concerns. The adoption of an authoritarian system relieves the distress of responsibility without resources.

In short, they rebuked their parents for having dreamed of freedom for their children, whereas their children would have preferred living in servitude.

Gee, ain't that swell.

GASPARD LOSES HIS MEMORY, PART TWO

THIS IS HOW it happened. One day Gaspard was going to his tub apartment. He was supposed to return early that evening, or later that night, depending on the number of linguistic pitfalls present in a Richard Brautigan text. The night passed, then the morning. Rose didn't fret too much. Gaspard must have decided to stay at his place, and she was aware of his aversion to the telephone. He had one—a cellphone—but basically never used it. In the late afternoon she attempted to reach him. *"You're exactly where you think you are. You know what to do."* The following day Rose decided to mosey on down to the tub apartment. No Gaspard, and the front door was unlocked. This time Rose started to worry. She called some of Gaspard's friends. Called me.

"I haven't seen him for a couple months."

She ended up going to the police station. They laughed in her face.

Several days passed. Then Gaspard woke up on a bench in the gardens of Versailles. He was covered in bruises. His head ached. He was holding a canvas bag whose sole contents were an apple and a partially eaten chocolate bar. He had no identification on him. Not the slightest idea about what had happened.

What happened to me? Where am I? What time is it? What's my name?

He went to the emergency room.

"What's your name?"

"That's exactly the problem."

150

They transferred him to Paris, to Saint-Anne Hospital, to the psychiatric ward. The nurses called him Mr. Versailles.

The National Health Insurance Bureau, the National Employment Office, the General Directorate for Internal Security, and the General Directorate for the Treasury, contacted one after the other, found no trace in their archives that might have provided a clue as to the identity of the unknown individual.

They then asked Gaspard to give the names of people and places, anything that went through his head. Those that he could recall, with great difficulty, provided no leads—until the day he said mine, a name sufficiently unusual to sound the alarm. As luck would have it, my last name's not Martin.

They looked for me. Found me.

I informed Gaspard—who didn't recognize me—of his name, the name of the woman he shared his life with, his job, his past. He duly noted it without really identifying with the individual by the name of Gaspard Boisvert.

GASPARD, AMNESIAC

GASPARD COULD NO LONGER recall his own memories. In order to reconstruct his life he had to refer to the two plywood suitcases, the voluminous dossier on his supposed Austrian roots that his father had bequeathed to him, the few articles that had appeared in the press when he assumed his position under the American President, and the memories of others. His mental stability and intellectual capacities were intact. He could read, write, be part of society. He remembered how to use various tools. He knew how to drive and to stop at a red light. He recalled his brand of soap. He was not unaware that sunscreen had to have an SPF of at least 30, unless you wanted to look like a German bumming around the Greek Isles. Yet even though he had not forgotten his English, the names of the authors he had translated didn't mean much to him, except a vague impression of having heard them somewhere before.

"A minor retrograde amnesia," the psychologist told him. "But your memory's still there. It has to be there. Imagine you're a computer. The hard drive's there where it belongs, but you can't access it. That's all."

Gaspard tried to imagine himself as a computer.

"Ah, memory," said the psychologist. "A real piece of work. It plays games with us our entire lives until we're on our death bed, and then it's game over."

Under the category comforting, one might have hoped for more.

ON TRANSHUMANISM

"Abolish death, oh ye mortal fools
Ye shall have a world composed
Of a bunch of immortal fools"

IN PURSUIT OF PROGRESS and following the example of the Christian Savior, modern man, thrilled with his evermore-perfectible immortality, was busy building himself a sepulcher where he hoped to live indefinitely, until the Universe disappeared, and perhaps beyond that. This was the primary attraction of new technologies that would make possible the transformation of man, living in an imperfect body, into a cyborg, an artificial, yet thinking, creature. The cerebral wiring would prevent this new humanity from quickly going dotty.

For want of the end of the world, the transhumanist revolution might have allowed the suspension of the laws of History that were heretofore in effect in order to precipitate the advent of a new man, following the model of a fully realized Nazi—strong, healthy, loyal, intelligent, friendly toward peers, and merciless toward degenerates. The scientific and technological revolutions of the past had already provided several possible directions. The printing press had brought *Mein Kampf, The Little Red Book,* and *The Global Islamic Resistance Call* into wide circulation; electricity, low-cost torture; and eugenics, organized extermination.

Similarly, selecting human embryos in vitro would have guaranteed a population of well-balanced and healthy individuals for society, each and every one equal. Finally, cloning the elements that had been perfected would have returned the world to the first years of the reproduction of living creatures. The division of a cell into an identical pair was until now the privilege of bacteria.

Innovative leaps and a return to roots—the two pillars of unabashed modernity.

THE VERDICT

"THE RESULTS, so to speak, are extremely clear. From a scientific standpoint, you have no link to the two Austrian DNA donors."

So pronounced Dr. Morelli. Only to add immediately:

"It is possible, however, that there was a father, perhaps several, who were not, so to speak, correctly identified on the family tree that has been circulating since 1703. In other words, one or two men in this genealogy may not be the biological fathers, the real fathers, so to speak, of their children. To be completely sure, it would be necessary to exhume the remains of Hitler's father, Alois. Then the proof would be irrefutable. That is, of course, if Alois is Adolf's father. Who knows with those goat-fucker Austrians."

The final sentence was pronounced *in petto*.

LINEAGE

ALOIS SCHICKLGRUBER, the One-who-dug-ditches-to-drain-the-liquid-manure, had had, during his first marriage, another son, Alois, aka Junior, who was therefore Adolf the Kraut's half-brother, and who himself had had a son who had become an American citizen, who had four himself—Alexander, Louis, Howard, and Brian. They all declared on American television that they had agreed not to have any children in order to put an end to this repugnant lineage. Now, granted, that wasn't a very American thing to do, and it no longer had any importance given the imminence of the end of the world, but all the same, it sure was swell of them.

THE END OF THE WORLD, AT LAST

"So, THIS END OF THE WORLD," said my editor. "When's it happening?"

"It already took place."

"Oh really?"

Sardonic.

"Yes. It's just that people didn't pay attention."

THE JOKE ABOUT THE TWO CHINESE, AT LAST

As for the joke about the two Chinese—I'd better admit to you now: I don't know the next part.

Furthermore, it wasn't even a joke.

Life's a bitch.

THE RAGUSA HOTEL

GASPARD CALLED THE WAITER, paid the check, rose, and, his steps slightly unsteady, slowly headed toward his breakfast-included four-star hotel featuring a shaded garden out front and a cozy courtyard in the back. A plaque above the entrance mentioned the names of several famous and forgotten people who had stayed there or dropped in for a vermouth—Francis Picabia, Marcel Duchamp, Tristan Tzara, Kiki de Montparnasse. The hotel was named The Ragusa, which was the old name for Dubrovnik, a Croatian city that had been bombed in the past by the Serbs. The Croats and the Serbs didn't like each other.

Rain fell from a sullen sky over Paris. That's how I imagine it.

Gaspard went up to his room. It smelled of cigarettes. That's how I imagine it. A cigarette was a narrow cylinder approximately eight centimeters long, filled with shredded tobacco and covered in thin paper. It was intended for smokers, who gave it affectionate pet names—cig, ciggie, gasper, smoke, loosie, fag. Smoking a cigarette meant slowly burning the cylinder of tobacco while inhaling the smoke through the mouth. Smokers were deeply attached to their cigarettes and couldn't imagine living without them. In the bygone days of the twentieth century, cigarette machines were placed in cities and towns so that smokers would never be caught without. In a short story by an author whose name I can't remember, there was a scene that went something like this: "We were pleasantly chatting when, overcome by some kind of rage, she violently headed off to throw herself at a cigarette machine, as if, without her smokes, she would peg out

159

within five minutes." Here cigarettes drive away death. But the doctors didn't give a hoot. First, they imposed harsh, threatening messages on cigarette packages, then an out-and-out ban. Gaspard purchased his cigarettes on the black market at an exorbitant price.

Smoking was, of course, strictly forbidden in The Ragusa Hotel.

Gaspard took off his blazer, laid it on the bed, and went to open the window. Overcome by vertigo, he wobbled, fell, and was impaled on the spikes of the metal fence below. He lived a few more moments but had died by the time the ambulance arrived.

This I learned from the doctor.

CONFUSION

"I KEEP TRYING to tell you. You're confusing the end of the world with the end of a world."

"Oh, there's a difference?"

"Don't act stupider than you are."

"It's just that . . ."

"With the end of the world, there's nothing after. With the end of a world, it's the dawn of a new world. Things change, you know. Everything changes."

"What for?"

"What do you mean what for?"

PATRIK OUŘEDNÍK was born in Prague, but emigrated to France in 1984, where he still lives. He is the author of nineteen books, including fiction, essays, and poems. He is also the Czech translator of novels, short stories and plays from such writers as François Rabelais, Alfred Jarry, Raymond Queneau, Samuel Beckett, and Boris Vian. He has received a number of literary awards for his writing, including the Czech Literary Fund Award.

ALEXANDER HERTICH is a translator and professor of French literature. His translations have appeared in Dalkey Archive Press's *Best European Fiction 2015, 2016*, and *2019*.